Starry Night

By

Wig Nelson

ISBN-10 0983314446
ISBN-13 9780983314448

This is a work of fiction. Names, characters, places, and incidents are either the product of the author's imagination or are used fictitiously. Any resemblance to actual persons, living or dead, events or locales is entirely coincidental.

Kevin Murphy never intended to change the world as we know it; however, he seemed to lose himself for just a short while and that was enough.

Acknowledgments

This work was inspired by the many science-fiction writers who gave me countless nights of mind-expanding entertainment. They showed me that nothing is beyond the limits of the human imagination and that sometimes it's okay to tell a lie – as long it's a good one.

I'd also like to thank one of my faithful readers, Erin Collins, for giving me a new idea for the ending of the book. Sometimes a fresh perspective can breathe new life into a storyline that begs to come alive again and end in a different way.

This book is dedicated to my best friend, Bogey, who sadly is no longer with us. He was the consummate beachcomber and is no doubt searching the beaches of heaven for another blue stone. Where there's one . . .

Also By Wig Nelson

Sirens

The Psychic

The Conga Player's Dues

Tall Tales Long & Short

Tall Tales Long & Short II

Jacks and Hands

The Little Shop of Lyrics
A Workshop

A Feeling of Power
The Musical

CD's By Wig Nelson

Fire and Life

Get There

Fools You Bet On

Soundscapes

Wigged Out

A Feeling of Power
The Musical

The Little Shop of Lyrics
An Audio Book

Starry

Night

Prologue

She was 3,700 pounds of pure female, and she was in heat. Her wingtips were twenty-two feet apart and curling up in a frenzied quiver, just enough to break the surface of the water. Her signals would soon bring a male to brush across her engorged genital region and release his seed. Then, there would be more of them. Giant manta rays gliding through the shafts of sunlight reaching down from the sky in a frantic oscillation like streamers from a maypole.

In time, they would grow to become massive creatures, not unlike living spaceships, with every movement like a symphonic expression of effortless connection with the world around them – water pressing over and under the sand-like surface of their skin, centering them in a personal universe. A certainty of position truly defined, without question.

But the great manta had more than a few questions on this night. She had feelings that were familiar and yet altogether new. She had mated many times before, but never with such a sense of urgency. In fact, if she wasn't able to attract a male and his desperately needed seed on this very night, she had resolved to dive to the great depths where the makos would have their fill of her.

It was all or nothing on this starry night. She would mate or sleep forever. There was simply no choice in the matter. Her mission left her both liberated and elated. She had never had such a meaningful direction in her life. Her creator was guiding her. She would do His will, or die trying.

Then came the dolphins. They had only a few feet of water to maneuver in because the huge manta was hovering beneath them and determined not to move. With the entire Atlantic ocean in which to swim, the dolphins and the great ray chose to occupy the same 385 square feet of space. The dolphins swam in a tight circle, breaking the surface just long enough to exchange their pheromone charged gasps of air. There was no thought of their safety, no consideration for their well-being. Their mission was before them. They had to procreate. Like never before, their destiny was a clear beacon to be followed without question. Soon there would be more of them.

They knew that the powerful new energy was emanating from the large alien shell that spookily held its position beneath the ray. They were deeply affected by the unusual energetic force field, but remained strangely oblivious to its presence. Indeed, life itself didn't matter beyond their unwavering purpose. They would obey this irresistible imperative without question on this night of nights.

After the dolphins, the sharks arrived. First it was the threshers and then the blues. Around and around they swam, taking care to avoid the dolphins who were in turn unconsciously avoiding them. They swam together for the first time in what seemed to be an eternity with a concerted effort to avoid any sort of confrontation.

Usually the two species gave each other a very wide berth, but on this night of pheromone frenzy, they blended harmlessly like the lions and antelope at a watering hole on the dry plains of Africa. Some instincts can be circumvented when survival is tantamount. The sharks had to keep moving in order to breathe, but the dolphins floated listlessly among them, like mindless marker buoys waiting for some regatta to tack around them.

Soon even the whales were moved by the urgent agenda. The right whales were the first to arrive. Their finely tuned sonar was able to triangulate the position of the alien energy signals from over twenty miles away. They were just about to begin their annual migration north for the warmer months of the year when the strange vibrations called to them and all but demanded their presence in the spontaneous dance of creation. After the rights, were the pilot whales and then at last the humpbacks and sperms.

They all circled in a lazy aquatic traffic pattern beneath the otherworldly shell like obedient aircraft following specific instructions from an air traffic controller. They were stacked according to size in a swirl of sea creatures, all in tune with the same powerful vibrations. They all shared one thing in common: an atavistic awareness somewhere deep in their evolutionary DNA, which was somehow familiar with these particular signals from their ancestral past.

Perhaps thousands of years before, a similar stirring of the alien shell first brought to life their desperate need to procreate. That sense of need was forever planted in their blueprint for survival, to be passed along with each successive generation until the sleeping craft once again was brought to life.

Finally, the flying fish, determined to pass through the same small bit of space above the ray, launched themselves like surface-to-air missiles over the whirling mass of sharks and dolphin. They only spent seconds above the miasma of sexual frenzy, but it was enough to draw them back, time and again, from all directions.

Soon the scene resembled a dome-like structure of layered sea life. Fish arcing through the air above the churning ocean, dolphins and sharks packed in a tight circle above the giant manta ray, while below, the whales moved in a sensuous swirl adding to the maelstrom. The sonorous mating calls of the whales completed the symphony of the primal mating sounds. Then, all at once it ended. The great ship that awoke from a timeless slumber slowly ascended and slipped above the waves. Its color was a dull green with patches of dark blue, which seemed to perfectly match the night sky. The whole craft glistened with seawater dripping from the hull.

After gently nudging the vast array of sea life aside, it slowly climbed up into the humid mist above the ocean.

It hung, ominously silent, six feet above the surface of the Gulf Stream, 90 miles off the coast of Florida. The sea life maintained their position beneath the craft, still intent on their selfless mission to multiply in number. There they remained for the rest of the night.

One Hour Earlier

Chapter One

July 6, 2005

7:26 P.M.

Melbourne Beach, Florida

"**M**isty, you want to go to the beach, baby?" Little did Kevin Murphy know that a simple suggestion to take a walk with his dog would lead to a chain of events that would change the very mindset of a hostile world.

The dog jumped four feet in the air, paws gyrating for balance on the way down. Kevin was always amazed at the way his dog could jump. *If only she could catch a Frisbee.* Misty was a very smart dog. Kevin never needed to ask twice when he mentioned the beach. Misty loved it. She would run like the wind, day or night, right along the edge of the receding foam. She never really got her feet wet. Kevin often said, "That dog is so fast she could run through a rainstorm and not get wet."

His house was just one short block from the ocean, so they could hear the waves clearly as soon as they stepped outside. He locked his door, and they started down the road for the beach.

The night was warm and humid, but a five-knot east wind made the heat a little more bearable. When they reached the dunes, Kevin reached down and released Misty from the leash. Instantly, she bolted. He was glad to see her stretch her legs.

Being mostly an inside dog, Misty didn't get as much exercise as she needed. Kevin knew it was his fault, but he was often too tired to walk her after a long day of work. The Florida heat can really sap a man's energy if he is forced to work in the elements for very long. July was one of the six brutally hot months of the year. The oppressive heat didn't really let up until the first week in October. Then you could look forward to very pleasant weather until just about the first of May.

Kevin had brought a few beers in a small cooler. He retrieved one and set the other ones under the stairs of the dune crossover. The air was infused with a salty brine scent from the seaweed gathered at the high tide line.

The hurricane season had taken away a good bit of sand, and the Army Corp of Engineers had been pumping it back in from roughly a mile out at sea. He made a mental note to comb the beach for Spanish coins when he got the chance in the hope that some of them could get through the filters that he noticed atop the hose barges. He knew that no one had yet discovered the treasure from the flagship of the fleet that was lost in the 1700's. *Never hurts to dream.*

Kevin settled down on his back to look up at the clouds. It was one of his favorite pastimes. He was always amazed at fantastic patterns in the Florida sky. He found himself imagining what lays beyond it. The boundless expanse of space sent his head spinning when he attempted to embrace its totality. Most people were content to define *abstract ideas* in terms of *absolutes*. But settling for pat answers like, *'Space is never ending — continuing on forever,'* didn't pacify Kevin Murphy. He was that rare breed of man who didn't shy away from impossible challenges. He felt that if he seriously applied himself to the concept, eventually, he would come to understand the boundaries of space. *Everything can be viewed as a whole if you encompass the sum of its parts. There are no exceptions. There is an end to space - as there must also be a center. Everything has a center - as well as a periphery.*

He saw a large meteor streak across the horizon. The remarkable brightness centered him somehow, allowing the boundaries of his mind to expand and fill with excitement. He tried to imagine where the meteor came from. Was it a casualty of some colliding worlds out at the edge of the galaxy? He remembered reading somewhere that Einstein once said, *"God doesn't play dice with the universe." Well, he ought to know.*

Perhaps there was a hidden purpose behind all of the seemingly random events. The two planets were supposed to collide. The meteor was supposed to end its long journey by landing in one of Earth's oceans. A man and a dog were supposed to be witnessing it on this evening as nothing more than a light show for two. *Why not?* he thought. *It's as good a reason as any.* Kevin completed the bizarre supposition by vigorously clapping his hands and shouting, "Author! Author!" as if God himself might suddenly appear and take a bow. Perhaps there was such a thing as pre-planned spontaneity, if you could forgive the glaring oxymoron.

Misty came back and settled in next to him, panting loudly.

"Have a good run, sweetheart?" asked Kevin. He reached over and stroked her head. Then he scratched between her ears. She got to her feet again and began walking slowly back and forth between Kevin and the shoreline. This was her way of telling him she wanted him to walk with her.

"Okay, okay I'm coming," he said to her.

They started south together, watching a summer storm far out at sea. The sky was just beginning to cloud up above them; however, about twenty miles out, the moon revealed a ceiling that was a dark, ominous gray. It was odd viewing such a violent weather phenomenon in complete silence. The lightning was furious. It would start at a point on the horizon and splinter apart in fierce fingers of fire, feathering upward and outward to the farthest boundaries of the storm. *Surely some of God's finest work,* thought Kevin.

Finding himself needing another beer, he turned around and whistled for Misty to turn back with him. She liked to walk about fifteen feet in front of him and would have kept on going if not for his signal. Good dog that she was, she turned right around and trotted on past him.

As they reached Third Avenue, Kevin walked up toward the dunes to retrieve a beer from his cooler. He put his empty in its place and closed the top. There would be no littering. *Ever!* Littering was for tourists, or sometimes, rowdy kids. Real Floridians always packed out their trash. *One doesn't foul his own nest* was his over-used mantra.

Kevin was sick about the impact that development had on the state of Florida. Primeval places like the Sebastian River snaked back and forth for miles with pines and palms crowding out the giant oaks adorned with their Spanish moss. He imagined that much of native Florida appears today as it did ten thousand years ago. Yet, a developer can clear-cut a dozen acres with a clear conscience and dig a huge marl pit into a lake to place houses around.

Then they somehow have the nerve to name their projects after the natural beauty they destroy. A tract named *"Tangled Oaks"* might have a few six-year-old oak trees, but they rarely saved any of the "great oaks," and the deed restrictions certainly wouldn't stand for anything tangled.

The two dusk walkers traveled north along the shoreline in solitude. Aside from the image of their two tiny insignificant specs on the huge expanse of the Florida coastline, Kevin also sensed some kind of importance in the grand scheme of things. The early evening at the beach could easily bring up these feelings. Somehow you had God's attention all to yourself.

Misty would keep going into the night if Kevin could keep up with her. She was in her glory. She seemed to be searching for something just out of reach as she tracked back and forth from the dunes to the shoreline. While he watched her weaving dance, Kevin spotted a strange object in the sand about 15 feet from where he stood. It emitted a cool dark-blue light that resembled the night sky out on the horizon. *Maybe the man-of-war are back*, thought Kevin. A couple of times a year the Portuguese man-of-war invade the Florida beaches. They look like shining blue balloons strewn across the sand. They're actually quite beautiful and alluring; it was an irony Hemmingway alluded to in *The Old Man in the Sea,* when he called them the *"Whore of the sea."* Although enticing, she can be deadly as well. In the case of the man-of-war, this jellyfish has very long tentacles, often fifty feet in length, which inject poison filled needles into the flesh of their victims. *In the case of women,* Kevin mused, *it's long tentacles of faith that suffocate you to death. They lure you into a mindset that depends on their honesty and then rip your safe reality from under your feet - but enough about Brenda.*

As he stepped closer, he could see that the object on the sand was not a man-of-war. Actually, it was the wrong time of year. They were usually brought ashore by more violent surf in winter. This object had a similar beauty, but it was definitely not a man-of-war.

It cast an eerie, dark blue light from its surface, which was puzzling because there was not enough light for reflection. In fact the night was comparatively dark now, aside from the occasional flashes of the storm on the horizon. He stood mesmerized by the object and the rhythmic sounds of the gentle rolling surf.

Through the misty dark envelope of the twilight, the blue object seemed to be emitting a light of its own. Not a reflection of light at all, but a *source* of light! *This can't be right*, thought Kevin. Maybe he was imagining something brought on by the beer. At any rate, it was remarkable.

The mysterious object held his attention, his eyes felt glued as though he would have to fight to break his gaze. Misty's bark broke the moment. She had discovered a group of fiddler crabs sitting up waiting for the moon to come from behind the clouds.

The crabs were much more active at night than during the day. Kevin supposed it was due to the lack of sea bird activity during darkness. He bent down to pick up the shining blue object to determine its weight. The millisecond that the stone touched his humidity-glistened skin he thought of Susan. He thought of her shape. *God bless the shape of a woman. What a wonderful gift of design.* Then he noticed the stone itself. *It's as light as air,* he observed when he finally exhaled. *Must be some kind of volcanic stone. Valuable? Probably not. But why is it giving off light?   Probably phosphorescence.   Maybe it's part of a toy that a child left on the beach.*

Again his thoughts returned to Susan. He imagined the two of them there at the shoreline sharing that very moment. The moment was as empty as a Sunday morning wallet without her.   He realized that there were things unsaid on his part. He needed to talk to her soon. Possibly even sooner than tomorrow morning, which was the agreed upon plan. When Kevin hosted poker night, she stayed at her mother's house.

Kevin placed the stone in his pocket, whistled for Misty and started back south.   There was no conscious thought to take the stone. There was never any question that he wouldn't. It was as though the stormy evening and all the events of the coming weeks were already scripted and his life just happened to be in the way.

Misty left the crabs sooner than Kevin expected. He usually had to coax her away from the animals.   Maybe she'd learned the hard way that some critters are better left alone. He thought about her getting a nip on the nose and chuckled.

"C'mon. They're gonna' git you!" he teased.

Soon they reached the Third Avenue dune crossover and Kevin found his cooler and went for that last beer. He replaced it with his empty and tossed the blue stone in as well. Misty stood before him with her tail wagging. He was glad she was so well-behaved. She dutifully waited to be put on the leash instead of darting out toward A-1-A.

"Such a good girl," he crooned.

Together they walked back to Kevin's house leaving the sand, surf, crabs and the storm behind them. Misty was as weary from running as Kevin was from the beer. When Susan was home, they all slept together like warm puzzle pieces in Kevin's double bed. He supposed that tonight, after the poker game, they would both be asleep as soon as their heads hit the pillows.

Chapter Two
July 6, 2005
8:56 P.M.
Melbourne Beach, Florida

Trust is a serious issue for most people, and Kevin Murphy was certainly no exception. It was very important to him despite his transparent efforts to play it down. Susan knew the difference. She could see the major stumbling block between where their relationship was now and where she longed for it to be.

Kevin and his other life companion, an English Pointer named Misty, were completely devoted to each other. Now, there is trust - dog's trust of man. It's totally misplaced in some instances, but nonetheless, an integral component of the pack-animal psyche, where a sense of security is assured by following the Alpha male.

Apart from a regular meal ticket, the loyalty instincts of a pack animal have a definite purpose in the world. If threatened, there is the assurance of a band of brothers and sisters standing shoulder to shoulder, if need be, in a battle to the death.

After all, what is life without honor and the sense of belonging somewhere that loyalty affords us? If only humans could learn the lessons of the so-called lower species. God's good intentions on autopilot. But man has to complicate things - oftentimes something as simple as trust.

Kevin did trust some things. He trusted that the sun would rise each morning out of the deep blue ocean in a bursting white light, that it would sweep across the sky all day and then crawl over the western horizon as a blazing red ball of fire. He also trusted that there were certain things that happen because they are meant to happen. He often sensed that he was living out a preplanned existence that he had somehow dreamed before. At times, perhaps, life experience is even co-written by an individual *and* that universal intelligence that shapes the primordial pool of matter and cheers it on. Free will exists only in the instance that it is already scripted. Perhaps there is such a thing as preplanned spontaneity, for lack of a better term.

These are the thoughts that entered Kevin's head as he and Misty walked the sand at low tide in the afterglow of the sunset. Often, when the moon's pulsating brilliance connected them through the ether, he felt himself to be a puppet dangling on the Earth and at the caprice of something otherworldly. They were just two souls on a lonely beach, one furry and short, patterning with four prints, and one tall and tanned, leaving a track of only two. On early evenings like this, their trail meandered through the wave-cast shore – chasing sticks and stray thoughts in the silence. But this particular evening was set aside for poker, and it was Kevin's turn to host the game.

There were five players seated at the table. The ancient air conditioner had lost the battle with the summer-baked roof tiles and had given up the ghost.

"Jesus, it's hot in here," said Mickey shuffling the cards. "Do you have the heat on, Kevin?" Mickey's bright blue Hawaiian shirt was gathering circles of perspiration beneath his armpits and across his pot belly. They resembled a silhouette of a much more famous Mickey who lived in a theme park some 60 miles due west of Kevin's house in Melbourne Beach, Florida.

"We might as well play outside," said Mike wiping his brow with the back of his hand. Mike had come straight from his job as a block mason and was still dressed in his work boots, well-worn blue jeans and a dusty, red tee shirt. He had a red bandana tied around his neck, which he untied and rolled up to make himself a headband.

"Good idea, guys. It's actually cooler on the porch," said Kevin, and he grabbed the bowl of tortilla chips and salsa off the table and opened up the sliding glass door. There was a slight breeze off the ocean one block away, and it carried the heavy scent of night blooming jasmine.

Bruce, the sixth player, hadn't arrived yet. He had the longest drive when the game was at Kevin's house because he lived in Grant, some twenty miles away. No one cared. They started the game anyway, "You're the small blind, Kevin – fifty cents to you."

Although Kevin was sitting at a table on his back porch in a house on Third Avenue, his mind was miles away. He kept replaying his conversation with Susan, although *confrontation* might have been an even closer description; *"Why can't you just admit you have trust issues?" she asked.* Susan's long brown hair was pulled back into a ponytail, which gave her otherwise soft and sensual appearance a look of stark severity. She always looked overly clinical to Kevin dressed in her lab-coat with the name, *Susan Lang, M.D.*, embroidered above her left breast pocket.

"I don't, that's why."

"It's nothing to be ashamed of Kevin."

"Who said I'm ashamed of anything? Quit being a psycho-analyst, Mrs. Freud."

"Come on, Kevin. That's not fair. You know that Brenda betrayed you. She stepped all over your heart. How could you ever trust a woman after that?"

"I can trust a woman. I trust you, Susan. You know that."

~

"Kevin! Wake up. Fifty cents," said Mike placing a dollar's worth of chips in front of his cards for the big blind.

The game was Texas Hold Em' which was becoming increasingly popular since the World Poker Tour started televising the games from Las Vegas.

"Did you order the pizza?" asked John-John as he wiped the condensation off of the large tumbler that held his rum and coke. As usual, he was dressed in loose baggies and a Tommy Bahama shirt which identified him as the local surf god, which he, in truth, happened to be. "I told you we could play at my condo, Kevin. My A/C is cranked down to sixty-five degrees."

"You'll live, John-John," said Kevin. "It's not that bad out here on the porch under the fan, and yes, I ordered the pizzas." He just couldn't seem to get his head into the game. His thoughts drifted back to Susan's complaint, *"You say you trust me, but not enough to marry me, right?"* she continued.

"That's bullshit and you know it," he had told her.

"Is it? How long have we been together?"

"I don't know - a year? Two?"

"Three years, Kevin! We know people who've been married and divorced already in the time we've been together."

"I just don't understand what the big deal is, that's all."

"I'm thirty-four, Kevin. Tick-tock, tic-tock!"

"That's not so old. You look twenty."

"Liar, but thank you anyway. Look, you know I love you. I know you love me. We both want kids, so what are you waiting for?"

"I'm ready any time you are. You don't have to be married to have a baby."

"Here's your lunch. I have to get back to the clinic."

"What have you been doing?"

"You wouldn't believe me."

"Try me."

"Dr. Singer has me doing marriage counseling."

"You're right. I don't believe you."

"See? Trust issues."

"Get out of here," he said laughing.

"Earth to Kevin! The pizza guy's here. Quick, pay him before you lose all of your money," said John-John.

Kevin was beginning to feel a little weary from the "instant replay" going on in his head. He got up and went to the door to pay for the pizzas, fumbling briefly with his wallet before handing the delivery boy a generous tip.

"What's with him?" asked Mike.

"I don't know. He was like that at work, too," said Billy. "He cut a piece of crown molding three times and it was *still* too short!"

Kevin walked back into the room where everyone was laughing.

"What's so funny?" he asked.

"You," said John-John. "Have you won a hand yet?"

"No, I'm still a virgin."

"Let's keep it that way," said Billy.

Everyone laughed again.

"Nice guys!" said Kevin. "Here I buy the pizzas and all you can do is give me a hard time."

"Shut up and go get the plates," said Mike.

Chapter Three
July 7, 2005
1:15 A.M.
Melbourne Beach, Florida

The rest of the game was more of the same for Kevin. When the clock struck eleven, he had only won two hands and found himself down about forty dollars. It wasn't the end of the world, but the money he earned as a carpenter was just enough to get by. For the next week, he would be feeling the loss.

In the game of life, however, Kevin was considerably more lucky. He had been dealt good looks and an easy-going personal charm. At a trim six-foot-one he weighed in at just over one hundred ninety pounds. His sandy hair and mustache framed his even features, and he often got more than his share of attention from young women at the beach or the volleyball games on Ocean Avenue.

He was well-liked and in turn could usually find something to like about everyone he met. His only bad luck happened at the poker table. Miserable cards! He had been on a losing streak for weeks. *How long does a losing streak last?* he wondered. His luck was terrible, but he never stopped trying. Maybe the next game would be different.

His failed marriage had not shared that optimism. He and Brenda had tried so hard to make a go of it. That deep heavy fog of uncertainty and failure that divorce can bring was finally beginning to lift.

He even had the good fortune to meet someone else. Her name was Susan Lang. She had shoulder length brown hair and hazel eyes. Her graceful tall five-foot-nine form would never fail to turn a few heads at the beach. But most importantly, she was a lot of fun to be with. This night he would miss her warmth in his bed. She was staying over at her mother's - her usual routine when the poker brigade invaded their house every sixth week.

When all of the players had gathered up their winnings and shuffled off to their cars, Kevin cleaned up the table and put away the remaining chips, dip, cheese and crackers. He was sorry there was no pizza left. He sometimes enjoyed it cold for breakfast the morning after a game. Misty liked it too and often sat at his feet with the steady devotional gaze that only a pizza-deprived canine can muster up. She was already curled up in Kevin's bed and, after turning off the lights and locking the front door, he decided to join her.

The Next Morning

Chapter Four
July 7, 2005
8:04 A.M.
Melbourne Beach, Florida

Kevin was awakened for the second time by a loud buzzing sound. He had hit the snooze button on his clock radio a few minutes earlier. He usually hit it two or three times, but not today. In fact, he was sorry that he automatically hit it out of habit. Now, he had to wait out the next three minutes before it sounded again, and he could hit the off button. Kevin had a *raging headache.*

"Oh, my head," he moaned as he tried to rub the throbbing out of his temples. Misty slept soundly beside him. "Never again," he lied. *At least I don't have to go to work today. That helps.*

Kevin needed three aspirins and a very large glass of water. Still, he waited until the alarm finally sounded again. This time he shut it off, making sure he steered clear of the snooze button. He made his way on shaky legs to the kitchen. The light was blinding. He knew he was going to pay for overdoing it the night before, but didn't think he'd feel this poorly. In fact, he couldn't ever remember having a hangover that was quite this bad. His head hurt, his body hurt, and he felt guilty for losing forty dollars as well. He knew he had to get his act together soon.

At forty-two years of age, he didn't bounce back as well as he used to. His ex-wife, Brenda, had left him a few years earlier, and since then his life was a poor excuse for killing time. But he had finally picked himself up out of that dark hole and couldn't afford to backslide now. He knew Susan deserved better than that. Better than he was acting for the time being.

His divorce settlement didn't require him to pay Brenda any alimony, which was fortunate. Actually, he was entitled to a small monthly payment from her, which he declined to accept, because her income was always considerably higher than his. But Brenda left him for even greener pastures or at least larger numbers on green pieces of paper. As it turned out, money was more important to her than living a peaceful life with someone she loved. *Thank goodness there were no children.* Not that Kevin disliked the idea of having kids. Kevin loved kids and was anxious to raise a few with Susan. He was just glad he didn't have any with Brenda. Brenda was too selfish to love anyone except herself.

But in those moments when he was honest with himself, he knew there was more. The "more" that he didn't want to face, the "more" that resided just below consciousness when he woke at night in a cold sweat to a dream that he didn't remember creating. Perhaps, it was someone else's dream and he had somehow stumbled onto the same frequency and intercepted some strange emotional baggage.

But that didn't really ring true. He was never very good at lying to himself, and this was no exception. When he searched his feelings, he couldn't even remember what drew him to Brenda in the first place. He couldn't remember anything that they really had in common. But the sex was good. There it is, back to the same old misdirection. Sex is often like some magic trick that turns off the rational mind.

He did remember feeling lonely and helpless in the wide chasm that divided him and Brenda the last months before the divorce. Somehow even though he knew that they were poison for each other, he just didn't want to let go - to admit that their relationship was a failure, that it had been doomed from the start. Perhaps, that was the reason behind his reluctance to walk down the aisle with Susan Lang. He never wanted to feel that way again - not with anybody. Ever.

But Brenda was now married to a real estate developer in Vero Beach, or '*Zero Beach*," as he sometimes referred to it. Naturally, Brenda said it was because he was jealous of successful people, but the truth of the matter was he was a bit of a reverse snob. Kevin often said, "I've never met a person with money who wasn't afraid of losing it." That fear seemed to dominate their lives. He imagined there were many fearful people in a place like Vero Beach.

Melbourne Beach was beginning to go the same road. Real estate prices had doubled in the past four years, and during the tourist season the traffic was almost as bad as south Florida. He couldn't shake the feeling that for one reason or another *Florida was doomed*. But that kind of thinking could do nothing good for a bad hangover, so he put his mind to more positive things. He thought of going down to Sebastian Inlet to do some snook fishing. A snook is the finest game fish in the world in that when you catch one, after a considerable battle most of the time, you can actually eat the darned thing. They were delicious, second only to a nice redfish! His mouth started to water just thinking about it. He only wished he were as skillful as he was enthusiastic. If truth were known, he often came home empty-handed. *Skunked* was the appropriate term for when you came home *snookless*.

Chapter Five
July 7, 2005
9:16 A.M.
Ninety miles off the East Coast of Florida

C aptain Ricky Saber was the owner of a shrimp boat called *The Seagull,* but most of the other captains sailing out of Port Canaveral referred to it as *The Dirty Bird.* Aside from the allusion to its namesake, the boat really was dirty, and so was its owner.

Times were hard for shrimp fishermen with catches getting slimmer each year and a steady influx of alien immigrants gaining Florida commercial fishing licenses. Saber would often say, "I'd be doin' okay if only I could learn to live on rice." He would always make sure that a person of Asian descent was within earshot.

All in all, there were very few people on the planet who would call Ricky Saber their friend. And that suited him just fine. Saber had no use for friends or even female companionship. He also despised the thought of a woman even setting foot on a *working boat* where real men made an honest living. His favorite saying was, "With a woman on board, you're a man short."

His unfortunate crewmembers were at the top of the list of those who had little use for Ricky Saber. Three poor souls dragged shrimp nets with him for two and a half weeks at a time. They went out about once a month and were miserable the whole time. Saber did his awful best to make sure of that.

He paid a generous wage, (the only way he could keep them on board), and he begrudged paying them even though they more than earned it. Their only saving graces were their cell phones and wireless internet connections. If it weren't for those small luxuries, Saber would have had an empty boat and bank account as well.

"I found it! She's mine!" screamed Saber from the deck of The Seagull.

"What now, for God's sake?" questioned the first mate, Adam Carter, to the other two men below deck. They usually ran the nets at night, attracting shrimp to the huge lanterns suspended over the side. Morning was best suited for catching a few winks as far as they were concerned. Now that idiot on deck was screaming like a banshee.

"I swear! This is my last run," said Tommy Hoffman.

"You said that last time," said Jojo Kale, the designated chef/shrimper on board. "'Member when I made the jambalaya?"

"I could handle that. It's *him* I can't handle," said Tommy. "Whatta ya' spose he's yellin' about now?"

"I could care less," said Adam pulling up his blanket and rolling over toward the moldy planking. *"Horse's ass."*

"I hear ya'," said Jojo.

"We just turned in about two hours ago," whined Tommy. "Man! Doesn't that guy ever sleep?"

"Can it!" barked Adam. "I sleep, and I'm try'n to right now, dammit."

"Maritime law! I'm claiming the salvage rights!" continued Saber in his bellowing banter.

"Jesus, I can't sleep," said Jojo. "I'm going on deck to see what the hell's going on."

"Have at it," said Tommy.

Jojo climbed the seven short steps up to the deck of The Seagull. Hoping to diffuse the moment, the ever-peaceful Jojo pulled himself through the hatch and said, "My captain, my captain. How can I serve you?"

"Look at my prize Jojo. *Look at It!* Isn't she beautiful?" asked Saber with his hand extended over the rail.

Jojo nearly fainted. Less than fifty feet away was what looked like a small cigar shaped *"something"* hovering at least six feet over the ocean.

"Oh, my God!" he offered to no one in particular.

"She's mine, Jojo," said Saber. "I saw her first."

"Are you crazy?" asked Jojo. "This is not some abandoned vessel you can claim. *It's hovering for God's sake!"*

"I don't care if she's crappin' in er' pants. She's mine," said Saber drunk with his new found riches.

"Maritime law states that if She's empty I can tow 'er in and claim 'er as salvage."

"You are a piece of work, Ricky. You know that?"

"Watch your tongue, Kale. I don't need you on my boat," challenged Saber. "I don't need any of you guys. I'm sick of the whole lot of ya' with your damned video games and clickety clack email to your sweetie pies," he hocked up a large piece of phlegm from his greasy throat and made a big production of spitting over the rail.

Jojo had no doubt regarding what he was witnessing. Saber had actually come across some kind of vehicle from another world. It hung above the ocean in an eerie silence, broken only by the swirling water beneath stirred by an unlikely collection of sea life. He could see sharks and dolphin, alike, swimming together along with what appeared to be kings, mahi, redfish and barracuda. They just didn't belong in the water together at the same place at the same time. It was unsettling enough to raise a patch of gooseflesh on the back of his neck.

Here was an actual flying saucer, for lack of a better term. Something no one in the entire world has ever substantiated with either a video or a photograph, and he wasn't even sure whether there was a camera on board to record the event. But something told Jojo that he wouldn't need one. This was no fleeting moment. The craft just hung there a short distance away and didn't appear to be in any hurry to disappear. His good sense took hold of him, and Jojo was instantly afraid for his life.

"I'm done, Ricky. Get me to port," said Jojo.

"We go in when the hold is full," said Saber.

"Come on, Ricky. Now you've got your flying saucer to look after. You're no longer a shrimp boat. Now you're an important man. Head for port before someone steals your thunder."

"I've got to get a line on 'er," said Saber.

"Perfect," said Jojo. He was an inch away from jumping ship and swimming home. It was summer and he liked his chances against the ocean better than against a madman, let alone what might be lurking in a hovering ship a few feet above the waves.

The responsible human that he was took control and he went below deck, "Adam! Tommy! Up! Right now! I'm not kidding! Your lives may depend on it! Look! I'm putting on a life preserver! I suggest you do the same. I'll put on some coffee, but *get your asses up and get on deck now!*"

Adam ascended to the deck and spotted the hovering craft, "Holy mother of God!" was the reply from a wide-eyed, fear-stricken face.

Tommy was not far behind and said, "Why aren't we moving? Get us out of here, Captain."

"Not on your life, Hoffman. Ain't ya' got no cajones in ya?"

"I've got a survival instinct, unlike you, Saber. Listen to this very carefully - I quit!" said Hoffman.

"Then you don't get paid," said Saber.

"I better get paid, or you'll never get a crew out of Canaveral again," said Hoffman.

"I'll pay you all just like usual - next week," said Saber.

"Ricky, we may not have another week," said Jojo sadly from the galley below. "Maybe we've never heard of that evil thing because no one ever survived to tell about it."

"What're you talking about Jojo? This thing ain't no big deal," said Saber shaking his rat's nest of a head.

"No big deal? It doesn't look like it's from Earth, Ricky. I don't think any military vessel can do that."

"All the better. Worth more money. And if she's abandoned, she's mine."

"It may not be abandoned," said Adam. "Isn't this the Bermuda Triangle?"

"Oh, don't start with that shit," said Saber. "There ain't nothing to all that Bermuda Triangle hooey. It's just bad storms out here, and every captain who knows what's what'll tell ya the same, Carter."

"Where the hell did it come from?" asked Tommy. "Did you see it fly, Ricky?"

"You call me Captain, Hoffman. I demand respect on my boat," said Saber. "No, I didn't see no flyin'. I came up on 'er 'bout twenty minutes ago and she ain't moved squat. Thought it was a storm cloud at first."

"That doesn't mean anything," said Tommy. "I say we should leave the area. What if it's about to start target practice, and we're the target?"

"Well, you don't have a say, Hoffman. This ain't no democracy," said the captain. "You boys help me tow 'er in an' I'll cut you in for five percent. Each."

"Five percent of death is still death," said Jojo savoring his cup of coffee as if it might be his last. He had just come back on deck and handed the other two crewmen mugs of steaming coffee.

"For Christ's sake, Kale," whined Saber. "Ain't nobody gonna' die."

"That's right, Captain," said Adam, "because we're going back in. And we're not gonna' try to tow a space ship. You got that?"

"I don't remember makin' you captain, Carter. Who do you think you are givin' orders on my boat?"

"I'll tell you who I am. I'm the only one on this boat who knows the gravity of this situation. We are in serious danger, Saber, and you're breaking the law by exposing us to it."

"I'm with Adam," said Tommy. "I say we leave now."

"Me too, Ricky," said Jojo.

"It's three against one, Captain," said Adam. "Have you at least called the Coast Guard?"

"'Bout ten minutes ago. Gave em' the Sat-Nav numbers n' they said they're sendin' a chopper and a cutter."

"When the chopper confirms it, they're gonna' send a few fighters out of Patrick, Ricky," said Jojo. "We might be right in the middle of a damn war. I'm sorry, Ricky, but I'm getting on the cutter when she gets here."

"So you're all gonna' jump ship - is that right?"

"Yup," said Adam.

"You bet," said Tommy.

"Ahh, you're all a bunch a babies," said the captain.

Chapter Six
July 7, 2005
11:46 A.M.
Melbourne Beach, Florida

Kevin had finished his second cup of coffee and brushed the cobwebs from his mind just in time to receive a phone call from his father. Kevin Murphy, Sr., lived with Kevin's mother, Judy, in a north Melbourne golf community called Suntree.

"Kevin! Have you seen it?" His father sounded as if he were about to explode.

"Dad?"

"Jesus, Kevin. Where've you been? Turn on your television. Channel six! Any channel, for that matter!"

Kevin found his clicker and turned to channel six. Skywitness news had the ship on camera, hovering roughly six feet above the ocean. An old shrimp boat was anchored nearby, which put the size of the craft in perspective. It appeared to be roughly one third of the size of the boat; nearly twenty-five feet from what would be stem to stern. The surface had a greenish brown hue and was mottled with patches of sky blue, giving it the appearance that it had been shot full of holes.

Kevin turned up the sound with the TV remote and heard the female reporter Carla Means speaking from the helicopter, "According to the captain of the shrimp boat

The Seagull on the lower left side of your screen, the ship has been hovering where you see it now for approximately two hours and twenty minutes. Although the ship appears to be able to defy gravity, Rick Saber, the boat's captain, has informed us that it has been dead silent for all of that time. It also seems on an equally curious note that the ship has attracted a variety of sea creatures to the area. The sea is literally teeming with life directly beneath the craft."

The reporter then switched off her microphone and asked the cameraman Ed Brownlow, "Hey, Ed, is it hot in here or is it me?" She slipped off her jacket and loosened the second button on her blouse. She fanned herself with a handkerchief that she had used to pat away the perspiration on her brow and asked, "Do you feel it? Jesus, it feels like all of a sudden I'm hot from the inside out or something. Does that make any sense?"

"Oh, I feel it alright," said the cameraman. His eyes shifted from her face to the cleavage she was suddenly revealing. "I think I'll shoot you from the neck up, Carla. I like the look, but I think it's a little casual for Ms. Williams' taste," said Brownlow referring to the anchorperson in the studio. "Are you gonna' be okay?"

She shook her head to clear her thoughts and buttoned her shirt again. "I don't know what's gotten into me, Ed. I'm sorry."

"No problem," said Brownlow.

She slipped her jacket on again and said, "I'm okay now, let's go again." She cleared her throat and the cameraman began to shoot the live feed, "We have roughly two hours of remaining flight time; however, we plan to refuel at Melbourne Airport and return as soon as possible," said Means. "We will be able to provide continuous coverage as we are awaiting the arrival of a sport-fishing charter boat called *The Gray Ghost* out of Summit Landing just north of Sebastian Inlet. Aboard *The Gray Ghost* is channel six reporter Bill Peters with a camera crew. They will be able to provide live coverage during the time it takes us to refuel.

"We have been given warnings to vacate the area by the Coast Guard helicopter that you see circling the strange ship. According to our legal department, at ninety miles off the coastline we are technically in international waters and beyond any jurisdiction of United States government entities.

"This is news, America. Big news! And Here at WCIX, we believe that *You Have A Right To Know!*"

"What's this all about, Dad?" asked Kevin.

"How should I know? Nobody knows, yet."

"How's Mom? Is she okay?"

"She's fine. She's always been stronger than me anyway."

"Is it aliens?" asked Kevin.

"Well, duh . . . ya' think?" his father, Kevin Sr., asked facetiously. "What else could it be for God's sake? The damn thing is hovering silently. I know the military has the capability to build aircraft that hover, but nobody can build a machine that's completely silent. It just doesn't add up. It's got to be alien, son."

"Damn."

"You said it."

The news team was circling the ship at a safe distance with the camera continuously covering the ship. The audio, however, was muted to accentuate the fact that the craft was silent. When reporter Carla Reams resumed her dialogue, the helicopter's engine could again be heard in the background, "So far there has been no evidence that we are in any danger. Standing by in our WCIX studio is anchorperson Shanice Williams in contact with retired Air Force General James "Buck" Sinclair by telephone. He is prepared to give us his assessment of the situation. Shanice?"

"Thank you, Carla. Are you there, General Sinclair?" asked Williams.

The television coverage was composed of a split screen with a live feed from the helicopter on one side and a still picture of the general on the other.

"I'm here, Shanice."

"General, tell us if you will, exactly what the mindset of the military is in a situation like this?" Ms. Williams could see herself on the monitor and was glad she had chosen a cherry-red dress with a low neckline from her wardrobe that morning. *Talk about a stroke of luck*. She had no idea that a story of this magnitude would break that day, and here she was in her Tiger Woods – power red –

Sunday best. *Well, what do you know; there really is a God after all.* The contrast with the retired general was driven home by the fact that he was fresh from the golf course, and thus, dressed accordingly.

"Well, that's hard to say," said General Hightower. "There is an S.O.P., or standard operating procedure for encountering alien technology, but it deals mostly with quarantine issues. Isolating contact. That sort of thing. As far as dealing with the actual ship, I'm afraid we're making this up as we go along so to speak."

"You're kidding, of course," said Williams.

"Not at all. If we are attacked, we retaliate. If we are sure their intentions are peaceful, we will try to communicate *our* peaceful intentions. In this situation we have to be very careful with our next move. In fact, my hat's off to the acting commander of Patrick Air Force Base, General Steven Hightower, for holding our forces in check. I'm not sure I'd be able to sit on my hands if I were in his position."

"Does that mean you would favor military action in response to this apparent invasion of our airspace?"

"We don't own the sky, Ms. Williams. When the craft finds itself over American airspace, well now that's a whole 'nother how-do-you-do."

"Can we expect our armed forces to fire upon the alien craft if it approaches the American coastline?" asked Williams.

"Of course, not. This is a small ship and we're not sure of its origin. It's really not much larger than your average SUV. I don't think it poses much of a threat to the citizens of the United States; however, if we feel compromised in any way, I'm sure we have contingency plans to deal with this object in short order. In other words, you can sleep soundly tonight, Shanice. I can assure you that you can rely on your armed forces to handle any threat from this particular aircraft."

"When you say you're not sure of the ship's origin, are you saying that it might be Earth technology? Possibly the Chinese?"

"It's not very likely. We like to think we're on the cutting edge as far as material design is concerned. I can tell you for the record it's not American, and, therefore, it's not native technology. In other words, the fact that there is no sound generated by its propulsion system means that the craft is very likely *not of this Earth*."

The camera cut away from the still picture of General Sinclair and back to anchorperson Shanice Williams holding a small ear-phone in place, "Excuse me, General. We have to break away for the time being. I am informed by Carla Means aboard the Skywitness helicopter that the Coast Guard is attempting to lower a man suspended from a cable down upon the hull of the ship. Back to you, Carla."

The control room switched back to the live picture from the camera crew aboard the WCIX helicopter.

"Thank you, Shanice. As you can see there is a man hanging from a cable beneath the Coast Guard helicopter. The cable appears to be about one hundred feet in length. Now the helicopter is moving directly over the craft."

The ocean was being stirred up from the downdraft of the Coast Guard helicopter but the strange craft remained eerily still.

"Now they're starting to descend."

The helicopter could be seen slowly closing the distance to the top of the ship. They stopped when the man was about ten feet away.

"The helicopter is now hovering steadily over the craft. Now they are beginning to pay out the cable. There he goes!" said Means, excitement evident in her voice.

When the seaman first touched down on the hull of the ship his feet slid out from underneath him peeling away a large strip of algae and seaweed. When he regained his footing, he dragged his boot back and forth across the top of the hull continuing to slough off large patches of seaweed. When the hull was revealed, it seemed to cast a sky blue light.

Kevin had the feeling that something was familiar about the craft. He told his father, "Dad, I'm gonna' hang up now. I'll call you back a little later. I don't want to miss this."

"Sounds good to me. Bye, son."

He turned up the sound on the television and pulled a chair up close to the screen. The control room switched back to the split screen of the live anchor desk and the still picture of the general. Williams continued, "Tell me, General Sinclair, what is the reason for the luminescence of the ship's hull? Would that have something to do with phosphorus in the seawater?"

"Possibly," said the General. "Or it may be an application of cryptic mimicry."

"Could you elaborate further?"

"Well, we sometimes paint our aircraft blue to blend in with a clear sky. The color may be a stealth application for all we know."

"Interesting," said Williams.

Luminescence, thought Kevin. And then it hit him. *A blue luminescence. Just like the stone.* He hadn't made the connection right away because the ship was mostly covered in algae. It must have been submerged for a long period of time. *Is there a connection?* He wondered. *And if so, what is it? Could the stone be part of the ship?* He retrieved the stone from his beer cooler from the night before to examine it more closely. *Susan, where are you?* The image of her body filled his mind.

When he walked back into his living room, he could hear excited voices coming from the television.

"It's moving! The craft is moving!" said Carla Means from aboard the Skywitness chopper.

Kevin stopped in his tracks. The seaman lost his footing and slipped off the side of the hull. The cable caught his fall, and he remained dangling in mid-air roughly forty feet behind the craft. The helicopter then gained altitude and the cable was slowly retracted, finally bringing the seaman back inside.

"Now it appears to be stopped," said the reporter. "It moved momentarily, but now it's stopped again. The Coast Guard seems to be breaking off their attempt to examine the ship's hull for now." Below the helicopter, the swirling maelstrom of sea life continued their frenzied dance of creation in movement toward the new position of the alien craft.

"General Sinclair, are you still with us?" asked Williams.

"I'm here, Shanice."

"We have all witnessed the craft moving. Can we assume that it is occupied, and if so, that we are in the presence of beings from another world?"

"At this point, I don't really feel that we have sufficient information to make that determination. By the condition of the craft, it looks like it has been beneath the water for some time. If that's the case, there may not be anyone still alive left to pilot it."

"So how can you explain its movement? Something must be guiding it."

"That may be true; however, it may also be on auto-pilot implementing a flight plan that was determined eons ago. Then again it's possible that the Coast Guard seaman triggered some kind of manual command."

"I'm sure I speak for the majority of our viewers when I say I hope that is the case. It's frightening to think that an alien might be watching our moves at this very moment."

Kevin reached into the cooler and lifted out the stone. It was warm to the touch. *Susan? When I reach inside this empty string of moments, I can only think of you. Half a soul . . . gently reaching . . . pleading for the completion that only you can give me. . .*

"There. It's moving again," said the reporter.

Kevin placed the stone on the coffee table in front of him. His mind began to clear.

"Now it's stopped again," said Reams. The dome of sea creatures again followed the movement and then came to rest beneath the ship.

Now Kevin was absolutely sure of the connection between the blue stone and the mysterious craft. He was also sure that he needed to be very careful with his next move. He knew that it could be possible to triangulate the direction of the apparent influence on the ship. He could lead the authorities right to his door if he wasn't careful. *Slow and easy,* he said to himself.

When he looked closer at the stone, he could see markings that resembled eight points of a compass on one end and two opposing arrows directly in line with the north-south axis on the each end. He touched the north needle of the compass symbol and nothing happened. *Susan?*

Then he pressed the upper or forward icon on the end of the stone. *Susan, where are you when I need you?*

"It's moving again," said the voice on the television.

Kevin then touched the south needle of the compass symbol and watched as the craft slowly turned a full 180-degrees. When he touched the reverse icon, the ship stopped. *Holy Mother!* He lifted the stone and pointed it downward and pressed the forward icon. *Susan, get home now. I need you now.*

He watched in amazement as the ship suddenly sounded creating a huge splash as though it were a great sperm whale and disappeared from the surface of the ocean.

"It's gone under!" shouted the voice of the reporter in the helicopter. "The ship has gone down beneath the water!"

Good place for it...for now, thought Kevin Murphy. *Where the hell is Susan?*

Chapter Seven
July 7, 2005
12:24 P.M.
Melbourne Beach, Florida

Kevin laid the stone down on the table in front of him and sat back, trying to take in the enormity of it all. He tried to grasp the full context of what happened during the last nine hours of his life - and failed. It was too much. The power of it was more intoxicating than any number of beers he could consume. *He had control of a space ship.   His own personal space ship.*

Not only that, he had his own personal television crew to teach him how to fly it. They would surely monitor its every move. He turned his attention back to the screen. Shanice Williams was still interviewing the retired General over the telephone, "What now, General? We know that the coast guard cutter *Sawfish* is en route to those SAT-NAV coordinates as we speak. What if the ship doesn't resurface? Will the cutter remain in this area?" she asked. "I would assume so, Shanice. They may have some success with echo-location," said the General.

"You mean sonar?"

"That's right."

"Are you aware that the Coast Guard has refused to let our camera crews board the cutter, General?"

"I'm not surprised."

"Why do you say that?" asked Williams.

"Well, for one thing, there is the liability consideration. If you were aboard an American armed forces ship as a civilian, we couldn't guarantee your safety. I'm sure your news organization's lawyers would have a field day if you were to come to any harm."

"What about correspondents overseas who might have to do their job in harm's way?"

"We're not at war with the aliens, Shanice."

"Not yet."

~

Kevin watched the television coverage switch from the split screen to the anchor desk in the WCIX studio. The attractive African-American woman was shuffling papers and appeared to be receiving information through a small earphone. "Back in five, Bill." She looked up at the camera monitor and said, "This is Shanice Williams back in the WCIX studio. Shortly we will join Bill Peters aboard *The Gray Ghost* en route to the site of the alien craft's appearance. Bill, are you there?"

Kevin heard the roaring engines of the large sportfishing charter boat. The picture changed from anchorperson Williams to Peters seated in the fighting chair.

"I read you Shanice. The seas are about a two-to-three foot chop, which allows us to travel at about thirty-five knots. That's roughly forty miles per hour so we expect to be on site in about an hour."

"Very good," said Williams. "Carla Reams and her camera crew are there now. They have another hour of flight time before they have to return to Melbourne to refuel. They plan to leave as soon as you have *The Seagull* on camera."

"I understand, Shanice. I'm told that if the ocean lies down at all we can get another ten knots out of this vessel, which will considerably shorten our travel time. We plan to sign off for now and get back to you in the control room as soon as we have the shrimp boat on the horizon."

"Thank you, Bill." The camera went from Peters to Williams at the anchor desk. "Carla, any new activity from the craft or *The Seagull*?" she asked. The camera showed Means aboard the helicopter.

"No sign of the craft, yet," said Means. "The boat is just lying at anchor; however, the crewmen are on deck and continue to wave to us. They're motioning something. I'll see if the pilot can get us any closer."

The picture of the shrimp boat on the screen became larger as the helicopter closed in. The men on deck were each holding one hand up to their ears.

"It seems that they are either talking on cell phones or they are gesturing for us to call them," said the reporter.

"Maybe the switchboard at the studio has one of them on the line."

"I'm told the switchboard has been flooded with calls," said Williams. "They probably can't get through. We'll try to track down one of the cell phone numbers for you, Carla."

"Thank you, Shanice."

Back at the anchor desk Williams said, "The men aboard *The Seagull*, which is a shrimp boat out of Cape Canaveral, have been trying to get in contact with our WCIX Skywitness helicopter by cell-phone. Our research department is contacting the Port Authority office to try to get a personnel list of the boat. We know she is registered under the name Richard Saber; however, attempts to reach a family member have been unsuccessful. Perhaps the Port Authority can give us a cell-phone number. Also, if any member of our viewing audience can be of assistance, please call the number on your screen. This is not the station switchboard. It is a separate number recently set up for this purpose only."

The number on the screen was actually Shanice Williams' personal cell-phone number; however, she was reluctant to give out that information. A few minutes later her cell-phone rang. She said to the television audience, "Please stand by." She answered her cell-phone and connected a speakerphone to the mike jack input.

"Hello. This is Shanice Williams. Who is this?"

"My name is Kristin Kale. My husband is aboard *The Seagull*. He wants off the boat as soon as possible. They all do."

"Your husband called you, then?"

"Yes."

"Is the boat disabled in some way?"

"I don't think so, but they want to come home. *Now*."

"I understand," said Williams. "Can you give us his cell-phone number?"

"Sure. It's 321-555-2937," said Mrs. Kale.

"Thank you, Mrs. Kale. We'll see what we can do."

"Oh, you can call me, Kristin," she said.

Williams chuckled and said, "Okay, Kristin. What does the captain of *The Seagull* want? Does he want to leave his boat for some reason?"

"Not that I know of," said Kristin. "He's kind of a jerk."

"Uh, well thank you Kristin for helping us get in touch with them. I have to leave you now," said Williams. She was well aware of the fact that millions of viewers were given the opinion Kristin held of *The Seagull's* captain. It was an uncomfortable moment for her in this, the biggest opportunity for an anchorperson in the history of television. She had to be very careful how she handled herself. She felt that she not only represented WCIX, but all African American television personalities as well. The pressure was enormous, and as a professional newsperson, she loved every minute of it. The control room switched back to the camera feed aboard the helicopter.

"Carla, this is Shanice. Do you copy?"

"Yes, Shanice. I'm here."

"I have a cell-phone number for you. Are you ready?"

"Go ahead, Shanice."

Williams gave her the number and Means said, "Got it. I'll get back to you after we make contact."

"Very well, Carla," said Williams.

Means dialed the number and Jojo Kale picked up on the first ring.

"Hello."

"This is Carla Means aboard WCIX Skywitness chopper, *Freedom*. Am I speaking to one of the men aboard *The Seagull*?" she asked.

"Yes. My name is Jojo Kale. I'm the one waving my hand at you right now."

Watching from his living room, Kevin saw the man standing on the deck of the shrimp boat waving his hand at the camera. Although he couldn't hear the conversation, he could tell that the man was talking to the reporter Means in the helicopter.

"Hello, Jojo," said Means. "Your wife called us at the studio and gave us your number. Are there any other numbers that we should have?"

"Yeah, Adam Carter's number is 321-555-9793, and I have and email address for you for one of the crew members. It's tomhoffmand@cfl.bs.com. Did you get that?"

"I got it, Jojo. May I call you Jojo?"

"Sure, Carla. I watch you all the time. You're good."

"Thank you, Jojo. Your wife, Kristin, said the crew would like a ride back to port. Is that correct?"

"You bet it is. Captain Saber wanted to tow the ship back to port if we could get a line on it, but we all thought he was nuts. We just want to go back. Ricky, the captain, will probably stay. He's after the salvage rights."

"That may be rather difficult if the craft is occupied. The pilot may have other ideas if you know what I mean."

"Well, what about our ride?" asked Kale.

"There's a sport-fishing charter on its way right now. It'll be here in about a half-hour. They should be able to take you off *The Seagull*. There's also a Coast Guard Cutter coming from Port Canaveral. You might also get a ride from them."

"Sounds good to me."

"So when did you discover the craft?"

"Captain Saber just rode up on 'er about seven o'clock this morning. The rest of us were below deck. I guess he just sort of watched 'er for a while and then he started shouting for us to come up on deck."

"Has the ship done anything that we would be interested in?"

"Nope. First time she moved was when you saw it, 'bout nine-thirty. Then it went under about twenty minutes ago as you saw."

"Any sign that the craft is piloted by someone?"

"Your guess is as good as mine, but I'll bet it's alien. It doesn't make any noise. *None at all.*"

"Thank you, Jojo. Hang up now and save your batteries. We'll get back to you with instructions about your ride back."

"Thanks, Carla. See ya."

"Shanice, are you reading me?" asked Means.

"Loud and clear, Carla. What have you got?"

"It seems that all of the crew aboard *The Seagull* would like to leave the area as soon as *The Gray Ghost* gets here. Can we accommodate them, Shanice?"

"I don't see why not. It's our charter. I'll tell Bill to make arrangements with the captain. Any sign of Bill's boat, Carla?"

"We can see them, Shanice, but they're still about ten miles off. We'll swing the camera around so you can see."

Back in his Melbourne Beach living room, Kevin could see *The Gray Ghost* as a small spot on the horizon. He turned his attention back to the ice blue stone sitting beside him on his coffee table. He lightly placed his hand on it and felt . . . *a calming vibration and, conversely, an excitation that focused his mind on Susan.* Although the feeling wasn't unpleasant, he felt as though direct contact with the stone compromised his judgment in some way, so he made a mental note to handle it with some kind of barrier or protection for his skin. Eventually, he settled on a work glove from the toolbox in his truck. It was almost totally effective, and his preoccupation with Susan was reduced to merely a *strong attraction* when he handled the stone with the glove.

He wondered how to make the ship accelerate and was immediately surprised with *the knowledge*. Of course. It was so simple. *Time interval variations.* He *knew* that when he touched the forward icon on the stone, it would move forward very slowly, and if he held his hand on the arrow longer, it would accelerate gradually. He also knew that if he repeatedly tapped the forward icon the speed of the craft would increase ten-fold. He *knew* he had to be very careful until he could skillfully pilot the craft by remote control. And by some strange form of assimilation, he also *knew* that only when he possessed that skill would the craft open up for him to climb inside.

That was a most appealing thought. *What a ride.* He tried to see if he could make the craft surface roughly two hundred feet from *The Seagull*. He lightly pressed the forward icon for about two seconds. He *imagined/sensed* the ship moving slowly forward under the water. After about fifteen seconds, he lightly touched the reverse icon and *imagined/sensed* the ship coming to a halt. Then he tilted the stone upward toward the television screen.

He mused that it was not unlike his TV remote that he used to change the channels. He barely touched the forward icon and watched as the ship broke the surface of the ocean, breaching like a huge, sky-blue whale roughly two hundred feet from the shrimp boat.

"The ship is up! The ship is up!" shouted Means' excited voice across the television. "There she blows!" she couldn't help herself.

"Can you tell if the craft is floating, Carla?" asked anchorperson Williams.

"It doesn't appear so, Shanice. It's on the surface of the water, but it's not moving with the wave action. It's sitting stone still like a very small island." I don't know how else to describe it, Shanice."

"I think we get the picture, Carla. Just hang in there. We all appreciate the job you're doing."

"It's my pleasure, Shanice. I'm just glad I'm able to cover this story." She knew it was the chance of a lifetime.

Kevin could now see both *The Seagull* and *The Gray Ghost* on his television screen. The charter boat was about two miles away and closing fast. The station control room switched over to the charter boat, "This is Bill Peters aboard *The Gray Ghost*. We're about to join *The Seagull*, a shrimp boat from Port Canaveral and an apparently alien craft at rest on the surface of the ocean. We intend to "raft-up" or briefly tie up next to *The Seagull* to remove her crew. Back to you, Shanice."

"Thank you, Bill. Carla, are you still with us?"

"We're here, Shanice. We only have a few more minutes flight time. After that we'll have to return to the Melbourne Airport."

"Bill is ready to take over monitoring the ship until you can return. What is your turn around time, Carla?"

"Only about twenty minutes, Shanice."

"Very good. Feel free to depart anytime, Carla. We have Bill's feed from the charter boat. He's just about there."

"Okay, Shanice. We'll be back in a flash."

"Bill, stay on the Bogey. Forget *The Seagull* for now." Williams was starting to relish her role as coverage coordinator.

"Will do," said Peters. For some reason, he couldn't get his mind off of his lovely wife, Camille.

Chapter Eight
July 7, 2005
2:28 P.M.
Ninety miles off the coast of Florida

Rick Saber was becoming more agitated by the minute. "If that boat tries to horn in on my salvage rights I'm gonna' ram er'," said Saber.

"Oh, great!" said Adam Carter. "Don't be an ass, Captain."

"Ricky, we're leaving. Our ride's here."

"What're you talking about, Jojo?"

"We're going to transfer to that charter boat - all of us. They're gonna' raft up to us."

"Like hell they are. This is still my boat," said Saber.

"You can't keep us here, Captain," said Tom Hoffman. "Give it up."

"I've had about enough of you, Hoffman, you weenie."

"Please let them raft up, Captain," said Adam. "Save us getting wet."

"Oh, all right, you sissies."

"Better to be a living sissy than a dea..."

"Can it, Tom," said Adam. "The captain has agreed to let us go. Don't push our luck," then he winked at Hoffman, "*you weenie,*" he added imitating the captain.

The Gray Ghost came up within hailing distance of *The Seagull.* The captain spoke through a bullhorn from the wheelhouse, "Ahoy, *Seagull*! Permission to raft up!"

Saber just raised his hand and waved them on. The men held bumpers alongside *The Seagull's* hull and the transfer took less than three minutes.

"Captain Saber. Will you be needing any assistance?"

"Nope," said Saber shaking his head. "I'll be fine."

When his crew was off the ship, Saber started his engines and inched up closer to the alien craft. When he was nearly alongside, he shifted the controls to neutral and began readying a large coil of rope to drape over the tail section.

"What's he doing?" asked the reporter Peters to no one in particular.

"He thinks he's going to tow the ship to Port Canaveral."

"Is he crazy?" asked Peters.

"Yes," came the unanimous answer from *The Seagull's* crew.

Saber was actually able to toss a large loop of rope around the ship's tail. He fashioned a huge cove hitch that would get tighter when tension was applied. Then he started his engines and slowly reduced the slack in the rope until it was straight. The shrimp boat struggled at first and strained against the ropes. Then the craft began to move ever so slowly. What the captain didn't know was that Kevin Murphy was assisting him from his house in

Melbourne Beach. He inched the craft along with the shrimp boat – letting the captain think that he was actually towing it ashore. It was a cruel joke, but Kevin wasn't exactly feeling like himself.

The feeling of power was intoxicating. He just couldn't help himself. He chose not to tip his hand yet, so he needed Saber to think that he was in control for the time being.

"The Seagull has successfully managed to tow the strange vessel for the time being," said Peters aboard *The Gray Ghost.* "This may indicate that the craft is empty. It's hard to believe that an alien technology would be powerless against an old shrimp boat."

"I'm sure we're all in agreement on that point, Bill. Stand by for a moment. I think we still have General Sinclair on hand. General?"

The television screen again showed a still picture of General Sinclair as he talked on the telephone.

"I'm here, Shanice," said the general.

"What do you make of the events of the last thirty minutes?"

"Well, as near as I could tell, the craft made no move to prevent that shrimp boat captain, Saber, from putting a rope on its empennage."

"And can you inform us as to what an empennage is?" prompted, Williams.

"The tail section of the ship. It's called an empennage. You'll notice that it has four fins instead of two rear wings and a conventional tail. Also, there doesn't appear to be any moving parts like a rudder or elevators. I see that as further evidence that the ship is unlike any aircraft on Earth."

"Would you care to elaborate, General?" asked Williams.

"Certainly. You see, a traditional aircraft designed to fly through an atmosphere is configured with a specific airfoil to accomplish lift. The curvature of the upper wing, or upper camber, is different from the lower camber, resulting in a difference of air pressure between the upper and lower side of the wing. It's called Bernoulli's Principle of Lift."

"Go on, General. I think we're with you so far."

"Well, if you'll notice the fins on the spacecraft, they're flat as a pancake. They don't create lift at all. That means that something entirely different is at work which enables the ship to defy gravity."

"That's a very good observation, General. What do you make of the fact that the *Seagull* is apparently towing the ship behind her?"

"It's hard to imagine that an alien would allow that to happen."

"Does that mean you believe the craft is uninhabited?"

"That's right, Shanice."

"Interesting. So why does an alien craft show up in one of our oceans with no one aboard?"

"Well, if I had to venture a guess . . ."

"Please do, General."

"I'd say that the craft outlived its inhabitants."

"I'm sorry? What did you say?" asked Williams.

"I'm saying that the technology lasts forever. The life force or pilot has a limited lifetime. This craft could have come to this planet ten or even a hundred thousand years ago. We simply have no way of knowing until we can get inside."

"Do you think there could be any organic matter that could be carbon dated inside the craft?"

"Again, Shanice, this is all conjecture, but yes, if there is organic matter inside, it can be carbon dated and then we will have much more information to go on."

"Thank you, General. Your insight has been very helpful to this reporter, and I'm sure to our listening audience as well."

"My pleasure, Shanice. I'll keep the line open and stand by if you'd like."

"Please do, General."

The ship continued to appear to be towed by *The Seagull* toward Canaveral Inlet. Kevin was going along with the charade in order to make them assume that the ship was *dead in space*.

He wondered what their reaction would be if they knew that a human was actually in control. He wondered if humans had the maturity and evolved wisdom to control such a craft. He wondered about himself, his own level of maturity and how this position of power was thrust upon him. He didn't ask for it. It fell into his lap by way of falling onto his beach. There he sat, able to control events that he didn't even have the understanding to grasp, yet. Unfortunately, humans didn't have the maturity and the evolution to match this kind of technology. He was drunk with his new-found power and he laughed out loud. Explosively.

His next thought was to explore the weapons system. The consummate pacifist, Kevin would never be concerned with weapons except for possible target practice. Now, he wasn't quite sure. He wasn't quite himself. If he were attacked, he very well might cause the ship to defend itself. *The arrogance of humanity. They might very well deserve a lesson.* This wasn't something that Kevin, the man, was looking forward to, but he had a responsibility now. It was a huge responsibility that he didn't ask for. But somehow it was given to *him*. He felt a change in himself that comes with the knowledge that whatever he did would have an enormous impact on his country and even his world.

He didn't want to lose himself. He didn't care a bit about the alien craft, and yet it somehow had a hold of him. He came to the sad realization that if he didn't have control of it, someone else would. That could pose a big problem for mankind. He wasn't sure of the capabilities of the craft; however, he had a strong impression that it was incredibly powerful. He knew by some undiscovered instinct that he could perform supernatural acts of nature with the help of this technology and even wipe out all of humanity with a wave of his hand. An incredible responsibility. *Didn't he deserve the respect?* Therein was the problem. His hand now trembled but he felt an excitement in his belly. He was awed and afraid at the same time.

Kevin's mind was well aware of the conflicted state he was in. He had to trust himself to remain in control of his emotions. He was wary. He was aware. He was jazzed. He couldn't just let it go. Maybe he had the answers. Maybe he could resolve the conflicts that threatened the world. The Palestinian conflict with Israel. The Northern Ireland conflict with England - the terrorists in Iraq. Maybe a spectacular show of might was the answer. He could certainly get their attention if nothing else. *Mankind could not ignore a swift kick in the ass.*

The first thing Kevin decided was that he needed to gain access to the ship's interior. He knew it would *teach* him what he needed to *know*. The ship could have a weapons system. That would surely be helpful. He knew he could never bring himself to harm anyone, but the threat of harm could be a very persuasive force. He explored the irony of *a force for good.* How can it be right to *destroy something for peace or* to *hate hatred*? Kevin understood baseboards and door casings and crown moldings much more thoroughly than world diplomacy.

He was conflicted by the morality of the situation. Did he have the right? Certainly the beings that developed the craft had the power to force their will on humanity. But had they? Had they held themselves in-check, or merely failed in their attempt to eliminate life on this lonely, insignificant blue marble in space? Perhaps a greater source of wisdom is a natural by-product of advanced technological achievements.

With luck, *restraint* would be one of the many things that the craft had to teach. He would only learn the things he needed to know by getting inside. He would spend the next few hours learning the movements of the ship by use of the stone. He lightly pressed the reverse icon and the craft stopped dead in the water.

The starboard cleat was pulled free from the transom of *The Seagull*. Saber felt the jolt and looked back to the craft sitting rock-still behind him. He turned the boat around in an attempt to re-attach the rope to the port side cleat. Suddenly, the craft took off.

It started slowly rising into the air and then accelerated almost straight up at a speed that was hard to imagine. The sonic boom was instantaneous. Saber instinctively ducked his head in response to the noise, thinking his vessel was being fired upon.

The camera aboard *The Gray Ghost* followed the movements of the craft as it raced back and forth across the sky. Breaking the sound barrier repeatedly, the craft created twin concussions, or booming sounds, each time it passed overhead. Then the craft quickly came to a stop two hundred feet off the port bow of *The Gray Ghost*.

"Maybe we should have stayed aboard *The Seagull*," said Tom Hoffman.

"I hear ya," answered Jojo Kale.

Adam Carter remained calm and said, "We're in no danger, guys. Saber's more dangerous than that ship out there," he pointed to the craft hovering ten feet off the surface of the ocean.

"What makes you so sure?" asked Bill Peters.

"Just a feeling. I think it's like kids versus adults. A kid will kill ants just for the heck of it, but an adult will only kill ants if he needs to. A kid does it just because he can. Whoever built that ship out there is no kid. If they wanted to harm us, we wouldn't be here talking, would we?"

"No. I guess not," replied Peters. He switched on a small microphone that was attached to his shirt collar, "We have just witnessed a number of aeronautical maneuvers by the space craft. There can be little doubt that that is exactly what we're dealing with here. Nothing on this Earth can duplicate the movements we have just seen. The sound barrier has been shattered from a standing start in mere seconds. Then from seemingly thousands of miles per hour the ship came to a sudden stop just a few hundred feet off our bow. It's this reporter's opinion that what we have just seen is a demonstration of the ship's abilities-intended to drive home the point of its superiority to any type of aircraft we have created on Earth. This may very well have been a wake-up call, Shanice."

The control room switched back to the anchor desk at WCIX studios, "You may be right, Bill," said Williams. "General Sinclair, are you there?"

"Right here, Shanice."

"General, would you concur with the comments from Bill Peters aboard *The Gray Ghost*. Do you think we have been given a show of force so to speak?"

"Well, there's no doubt we've been given a show of force. I can assure you that our Air Force doesn't possess any aircraft that can perform any of those maneuvers. However, the intention of the display is still a mystery to me. It just doesn't wash."

"I'm sorry, General. Could you be more specific? I'm not sure I understand what you're saying," said Williams.

"A technology like this has no need to flex its muscles if you know what I mean. We know they're superior. They know they're superior. What do they gain by showing off? Nothing. It just seems to me that the technology doesn't match the behavior."

"Interesting," said Williams. "Could it be a response to the attempts of Captain Saber to tow the ship ashore?"

"Possibly, Shanice, but I have a feeling that the ship could squash that shrimp boat like a bug if it really wanted to. I'll bet it was oblivious to Saber's actions."

"You sound like there is a consciousness connected with the actions of the spacecraft."

"There's no doubt about it," said the General. "Someone is in control. The maneuvers are not some predetermined reaction programmed into the hardware. What we have just witnessed is deliberate action, especially the return to the fishing boat. It may be an invitation to open a line of communication with us."

"And how would you go about communicating with the craft."

"Well, you might try talking to it," said the General.

"Talking to it," repeated Williams somewhat confused.

"Sure. Take out a bullhorn and say, *'Ahoy, Spacecraft!'* What could it hurt?" asked Sinclair.

"Nothing, I guess. Bill, did you hear the suggestion from General Sinclair?" she asked Peters.

"I heard it, Shanice," said Peters.

"What do you think, Bill?"

"It may be worth a try. We're going to try to get a little closer." Peters turned away from the camera and said to Jim Morton, the boat's captain, "Jim, can you bring us in a little closer?"

"Sure, Bill," said Morton. "But not too close. Remember, I'm just the captain. I don't own this boat."

"Understood, Jim."

Morton moved the sixty-five foot Hatteras slowly closer to the craft that was still hovering above the waves. He stopped when they were about eighty feet away. He shifted both engines into reverse and gave them a short burst. He wanted to demonstrate that he didn't intend to close the distance any more than they already had.

Peters raised the bullhorn and said, "Ahoy, there. We are a television crew photographing your ship. Do you understand?"

The craft remained silent. *Absolutely silent.* Peters turned back to the camera and said, "I feel kind of silly." He tried again, "Ahoy! We would like to communicate with you. Will you follow us to shore?" asked Peters.

Again, silence from the craft. And then it went back under.

"It's gone down again, Shanice," said Peters.

"We could see it, Bill," said Williams. "Any sign of it at all, Bill? Maybe just under the surface?"

"We're closing in now, Shanice, but so far we can't see a thing."

"Stay with it, Bill. Carla is due back any minute. They might be able to get some kind of an image from higher up."

"This is Carla Means, back on site of the craft appearance. We're closing in on *The Gray Ghost* now. We've monitored their transmission back to you, and we saw the ship go under. We're right over the location where she went down. Can you see it, Shanice?"

"We're getting a good feed, Carla. The camera work is excellent, but we can't see anything. Can you?" asked Williams.

"I'm sorry, Shanice. We don't see anything."

"Well, stay on site as long as you can. Send us the arrival of the Cutter when she gets there."

"Will do," said Means.

The ship would make no more appearances that day. It was safely put to rest three-hundred-sixty feet beneath the surface of the ocean. There was only one person who knew the whereabouts of the mysterious ship. He was quietly sipping a cup of coffee in his Melbourne Beach living room. His life was about to change.

Chapter Nine
July 8, 2005
1:13 A.M.
Indialantic, Florida

Kevin stood on an isolated stretch of beach in a little town called Indialantic, Florida. It was only about three miles north of his home, but the lack of condominiums and single-family houses meant that the beach would be completely dark except for the light of the moon and stars.

He wouldn't have been surprised to see a loggerhead turtle laboring up to the dunes to lay her eggs. It was a common sight amid the darker stretches of beach. They were magnificent animals, only four feet in length, and weighing over six hundred pounds.

Fifty-five days after laying her eggs, over a hundred hatchlings would climb out of the sand and make their way to a moonlit sea. Only about three percent would survive to maturity; however, those lucky ones would enjoy a life of over two hundred years.

Tonight, there wasn't a soul on the beach, neither human nor reptile. The setting was just right for the silent arrival of an alien spacecraft on a lonely Florida beach. He looked around him one last time. He was alone.

Kevin raised the stone and pressed the forward icon. *Susan, I wish you could be here with me now. . .* He *knew* the ship had broken the surface of the ocean. He then leveled the stone and pressed the symbol for due west and then once again pressed the forward icon. He tapped the icon a few times to speed up the ship. For the first minute nothing happened. He wasn't sure of the speed at which the ship would be arriving so he lightly tapped the reverse icon to slow the ship down.

Soon he began to hear a low rumbling sound beneath his feet. The ground was growling in a huge low-pitched vibration. At first he didn't understand and then the realization hit home. *The curvature of the Earth. Ninety miles out to sea is below the horizon.* He had retrieved the ship *through* the surface of the Earth. He quickly pressed the symbol for east and tapped the forward icon. He continued to hear the grumbling sound as the ship slowly made its way back out to sea. He then pressed the reverse icon to stop the ship somewhere off the coast. *Enough for tonight.*

Realizing that he may have drawn unwanted attention to the area, Kevin left quickly. Upon reaching his home, he cracked a beer and sat down on his couch to consider his next move. *Big mistake, Kevin.*

~

July 9th

9:05 A.M.

Melbourne Beach, Florida

"Kevin! It's Christmas at two-roads!"

"John-John? Is that you?"

"Get your board and head on down, buddy.   It's Christmas at Two-Roads!"

"What are you talking about?" asked Kevin.

"For the first time ever there's a right break *and* a left break. It's better than Sebastian."

"Are you sure? You've seen it?"

"I'm there now, Kevin. I've been going left all day. It's the sweetest little A-frame I've ever seen. I haven't had a good left since Barbados. Grab your board and come on down!"

Two-Roads was the name of the section of beach Kevin had been to the night before. Apparently the ship had dredged a trough under the shore that must have collapsed, and for the time being created waves that broke both left and right. It was a surfer's paradise. John-John ought to know. He'd surfed the most spectacular waves in the world on the pro circuit.

Eventually, the sand and coquina shells would fill in the depression and things would be back to normal. Kevin hung up the phone and said, "Glad to be of service," but there was no one on the phone to hear him. John-John was already paddling out to catch the next wave.

~

Susan Lang, after pulling a ten hour shift at the Mental Wellness Clinic, stumbled heavily through the service door which led from Kevin's garage into the kitchen. She threw her notebook and portable tape recorder on the countertop and crossed the room, retrieving a beer from the refrigerator.

"Beer for breakfast?" said Kevin.

"It's breakfast for you, Kev. For me it's cocktail hour. I went to work at ten o'clock last night. So, what do you think?"

"About what?" he said absently. *Wasn't there something he wanted to tell her? For some reason it slipped his mind.*

"What do you mean, about what? The aliens, Kevin." Susan shook her head and a stream of exasperation escaped her lips, "Jesus, what's wrong with you. In case you haven't noticed, the sky is falling and we're all a little chicken."

"That's good," he said. "Little chicken," he repeated chuckling.

"It's nothing to laugh at, Kevin. Aren't you just a little bit scared?"

"Not really. I think the ship is empty, Susan."

"Oh, that makes me feel a lot better. This alien – *machine* – has got a mind of its own, that's just wonderful."

Kevin had intended to tell Susan of his discovery of miraculously stumbling upon a control stone for the strange craft, but for some reason he now chose to keep it to himself.

Susan could hear the continuing news broadcast in the living room, and she left the kitchen with her half empty beer to rejoin the historical cataclysm. Kevin heard her calling back over her shoulder, "Where's Misty?"

"What?" said Kevin walking up behind her.

"What do you mean, what? The dog, Kevin. Where's Misty?"

"Uh, I guess she's not here."

"You guess? What's the matter with you? Every time I come into this house, Misty is here waiting – telling me she misses me – demanding her scratch on the head – being the regular pain in the ass she always is - and you don't notice that she's not here? Have you looked outside?"

"She's an inside dog."

"That's the point, Kev. Where's the fucking dog?"

"I don't know."

"Well, that's just great. You don't know. Jesus, Kevin."

"I'll look in the yard," he said weakly.

"Don't bother, asshole," she slammed her beer down on the coffee table, and the foam cascaded down the side of the bottle to the magazine beneath it. Kevin stood staring at the television set trying to remember something at the edge of his mind. Something important. It had to do with Susan, but it was just out of reach. *Oh, well, it will probably come back to me later.*

Susan walked heavily to the backyard sliders and wrenched the door aside to look outside. "She dug out again, Kevin." said Susan closing the door.

"Oh."

"That's it? Oh? Don't you want to go looking for her? She's your dog for Christ's sake."

"Okay," he said absently. He couldn't get his mind on a specific thought. It was like he was drifting across multiple images and couldn't assign any order of importance to any of them. *The dog is missing – I need to tell Susan something – This ship, or whatever, has something to do with the stone I found on the beach last night – I should tell her - should I tell her? – can I trust her? – What the hell is happening – and why is it happening to me?*

"Singer asked me to go to Dave Matthews with him and I'm going."

"What?" he asked.

"Listen closely, Kevin. Next Friday night you may or may not notice that I'm not home - *if* you happen to look around the house. And just in case you might wonder *where* I am - *if you happen to notice that I'm not here,* I'm telling you now that my boss, Doc Singer has asked me to go to the Dave Matthews concert over in Tampa. It's not a date or anything; he's just trying to be nice."

"Uh huh."

"He said he tried to get a ticket for you, too, but you know how the Dave heads are. The tickets were gone in about two minutes after they starting selling them."

"Okay."

"Kevin, are you alright?" she asked.

"Sure," he said.

"Aren't you worried about Misty?"

"She'll come back," he said.

"Aren't you worried about me?" she asked jokingly.

"You'll come back, too," he said vacantly.

Susan shook her head and peeled her shirt off walking out of the living room and down the hall. He heard her small voice off in the distance, "I'm going to shower. Come get me if anything happens on the TV."

Chapter Ten
July 11, 2005
8:55 P.M.
West Melbourne, Florida

The next time Kevin attempted to retrieve the ship, he was considerably more successful. The following Friday night he drove west on State Road 192 across the Melbourne Causeway and continued for about twelve miles. He then turned south onto a dirt road and traveled another two. The land was nearly unpopulated in that area. There were only cows and birds in the wide pasture in front of him. He knew it was just a matter of time before the Air Force would zero in on the motion of the ship. He had to complete his actions in a very short period of time.

He pressed the forward icon and raised the stone until it pointed at a forty-five degree angle due east. He *imagined* the ship rising out of the ocean. Then he brought the stone straight over his head. Instantly, he heard the sonic boom far overhead as the ship completed the arc from far out to sea to directly over the pasture. Quickly he tapped the reverse icon and watched intently for signs of the ship. He saw it closing quickly on the pasture and tapped the forward icon to slow its descent. When it was nearly on the ground he slowed it to a stop and lowered the stone forward to make the ship horizontal.

It was immaculate. There was not a trace of seaweed or algae on the ship any longer. Apparently, the extreme speed produced enough heat to sterilize the exterior of the craft. The blue light was darker to match the night sky. It was generated from deep inside the ship, and its effect was extremely tranquilizing. He had to keep his wits about him. It wouldn't be long until he was located by a triangulation of the ship's trajectory.

He walked forward with the stone. The ship stood still. On the port side of the hull near the center was an indentation that exactly matched the size and shape of the stone. An awareness, very deep in his mind, told him that he should expect to find and an identical indentation on the starboard side as well. He placed the stone into the portside cradle and instantly heard the break of an airlock that sealed the ship. Soon, a gentle hissing sound escaped as the skin on the forward section began to slide back into a crevice revealing a small cockpit inside the ship. There were two chairs positioned side-by-side with another permanently affixed control stone between them.

The blue surface of the hull was not smooth as he imagined, but rather rough as though covered by a huge piece of fine sandpaper. When Kevin wondered why the surface was rough the answer *became* a part of his memory. Each particle of sand reacted to the magnetic fields of any given celestial body. Unlimited power! The movements of the stone attracted or repelled the magnetic attractions. *Magnetism as a source of propulsion! Incredible!*

Kevin wasted no time, though he cautiously climbed down into the cockpit of the ship. When he was seated, the ship's canopy began to close, and he noticed the control stone sink into the side until it completely disappeared. There was indeed another indentation on the starboard side of the hull, but it appeared to be empty. He wasn't sure how he knew, but he was sure that the portside stone would not work on the starboard indentation. When he *reached out* with his mind, he *expected* to be told the location of the starboard stone, though the ship was strangely silent.

When he placed his hand on the stone next to the seat, he felt a tingling as though his hand had been asleep, and he was now feeling the pins and needles sensation of it waking up. He wondered briefly what the feeling meant and the image of a double helix filled his mind. *Something about DNA,* he reasoned. He reached out with his mind for the answer and a downpour of understanding filled his cistern mind. He knew that his DNA was deposited into the craft as a security measure and only he could gain access to the ship's interior.

He also knew that a string of previous DNA strands had been deposited in the ship over time and that it would automatically reset itself when it could no longer detect his life force. *As long as I am alive, no one else can enter the ship without me. Perfect.*

He pulled up slightly, and the ship began to rise. He then pressed the forward icon and was gently pushed back into his seat. Although he was accelerating at an enormous rate of speed the ship somehow counteracted the G-forces that it produced.

He saw the lights beneath him moving quickly by and out of sight. He *became* the meteor that had given him a sense of center just a few short days earlier on the beach with Misty. Instead of merely witnessing God's best work, he began to have the notion of being God's best work. Beneath his hand were life and death and consequences surely beyond any measure.

Words couldn't begin to describe his feelings. The sheer power at his fingertips was an awesome totality to comprehend.

It was the word for which there was no word. It was the Tao. It was Buddha. It was Job. It was God. He was intoxicated by the power and clearly bound for madness.

A spherical view-screen was activated all around him, and he found that when he concentrated on a specific area, the picture would automatically zoom in for him. A ventilation system awoke from a near century-and-a-half of hibernation. He could sense the presence of a previous pilot named, curiously, *Coal-Eyed Joe*.

As the Earth fell away beneath him, he was surprised to learn that the Earth's gravity had little or no effect on the ship. It was instead in concert with thousands of interconnecting magnetic forces as near as Earth's moon and as far away as her sun.

Another surprise was the silence of the ship's operation. He heard neither the fierce pressure of the ship's hull being forced through the atmosphere nor the sonic boom that it surely left in its wake.

Kevin knew it was only a matter of time before his sanity would become seriously compromised. Every exhilarated fiber of his being was on an indescribable high. As he pulled wildly up and pushed fiercely forward on the icon, the Earth quickly fell away behind him. In minutes he found himself rapidly approaching Earth's moon. A hideous laughter escaped him. It was uncontrollable. *Immortal laughter.*

Kevin decided that he didn't need a ticket, after all, to attend the Dave Matthews concert. He *knew* that the ship's stealth properties would allow him to hover silently above the concert venue in Tampa, and no one could detect his presence.

~

Misty was trotting south along A-1-A. She stayed close to the shoulder of the road although she didn't seem to be affected by the cars. She had dug a hole under the fence behind Kevin's house back on Earth. She was looking for a new place to settle. Perhaps she could find a whole new family to love. Somehow she knew she wouldn't like immortal laughter.

~

July 11, 2005
Raymond James Stadium
Tampa, Florida

Kevin eased the ship over the 50 yard line at an altitude of roughly twenty-six feet. He was only forty feet from the stage that was miraculously constructed on the field in less than three hours. Dave Matthews was lurking silently in the wings, checking out the audience as was his usual practice before a show. At first he seemed to be yet another of the roadies, moving mic stands, drinking beer, turning a myriad of dials on the monitor speakers after picking up a guitar and strumming an experimental sound check.

It was all unnecessary, of course, because there was any number of support personnel who traveled with the tour for just those purposes; however, Dave was not your ordinary musician. It seemed like he always ascended beyond the physical circumstance *in his mind* where he was not only the performer, but also the audience as well. The luxury of being in the position to be taken seriously for his much-rehearsed self expression was exactly where he needed to be. He never took it for granted, and, therefore, projected the appearance to be merely one of the masses, albeit the one *behind* the microphone.

Kevin was scanning the crowd beneath him when he noticed a rather peculiar turn of events. A very shapely co-ed right beneath the ship abruptly shed her shirt over her head revealing the fact that there was nothing but mother-nature underneath. She then quickly grabbed the handsome young man beside her and placed his hands on her breasts. It didn't take long for the young man to discern the young lady's intentions as he immediately loosened his belt, unzipped his fly and dropped his pants.

A few scattered applause ensued from the immediate surrounding seats; however, they quickly abated as the mood proved to be contagious in that the concert goers in the roughly fifty foot radius were quick to join in on the frenzied act of spontaneous sex.

Kevin had been to dozens of concerts over the past fifteen years; however, he had never witnessed such a brazen sexual display as he was seeing on this night. There seemed to be a desperate energy behind the acts, almost as if they were not meant to be as pleasurable as they were to be - *consummated*. Indeed, he noticed that the participants were not actually smiling as he expected them to be, and they were almost expressing a desperate relief when the acts were completed.

Then he noticed Susan. She was naked from the waist up and lying on her side in the grass with a hap-hazard pile of folding chairs beside her. Doctor Singer was prone on the grass, as well, with his pants down comically to his ankles as though someone had pulled them down and caused him to fall on his face. The small group of people beneath Kevin in his silent and invisible craft were well beyond any sense of modesty or propriety. They were completely oblivious to the fact that others were watching them fornicate and remained, for all intents and purposes, naked after the fact.

His thoughts turned to Woodstock, but even Woodstock was never actually that – *wanton*. It made him think of witches and warlocks around a bonfire deep in the woods, daring a vengeful God to strike them down for their indiscretions.

Kevin was furious. He was told by Susan that her boss, that asshole, *Doctor (I need you to work ten hour shifts)* Singer had no interest in her other than rewarding her hard work at the clinic. It didn't take a rocket scientist to understand he had just had sexual intercourse with Susan, and she was certainly a willing participant. His first impulse was to punish them for their treachery, and then the ship caught hold of his mind and reined him in. It left him with a feeling of pity rather than vengeance.

Matthews, seemingly taken aback by the virtual sea of oblivious id, seized the microphone at center stage and said, "I see the sex, man, but where is the love?" A chuckle began to reverberate through the crowd like a wave during a Buc's game and nervously abated as they came to realize that the performer was clearly not amused. Indeed, Matthews was unsettled and annoyed at the small section of the audience who seemed somehow removed from the rest of the humanity around them. It was as though he felt their sexual display cheapened the venue that was so sacred to him, allowing him to impart his message to a sophisticated group of people who called themselves *Dave heads*.

Kevin could relate to the feelings of the artist. He was particularly annoyed, but for a different reason. He felt betrayed by one of them. The next emotion he felt was relief for the fact that he hadn't shared his wonderful secret with her. Perhaps he wouldn't be able to share it with anyone, ever. It was a small price to pay, actually, for the incredible responsibility that was suddenly thrust upon him. He sensed it was not entirely by chance, and certain events and realizations in his life have been *steering* him to this very circumstance. Kevin was determined to be a good steward as the Bible had charged him to be. But he was also very alone.

Chapter Eleven

July 12, 2005

10:15 A.M.

Ninety miles off the East Coast of Florida

The Coast Guard Cutter *Sawfish* arrived on the sight of the alien ship's appearance about an hour too late. The ship had gone under and wouldn't appear again for more than five days. Fighter aircraft were also deployed to the area from the Air Force base in Satellite Beach, but had made no contact with the craft so far.

Rick Saber was still anchored in the area and had agreed to accept a WCIX news team aboard his boat for an exorbitant fee. *The Gray Ghost* had returned to Summit's Landing on July 7th, five days earlier, leaving Bill Peters and his cameraman to rough it aboard *The Seagull*. The accommodations were clearly a step down from the *Gray Ghost*, and there was no guarantee that the ship would ever resurface in that area. In fact, the only reason that it finally did was because Captain Saber unwittingly forced the issue.

One of his favorite pastimes was shooting his mini-14 assault rifle at dolphins. He claimed they ruined his shrimp nets, but none of his crew could ever corroborate that claim. On the morning of July 12th, Saber was once again on deck with his gun taking shots at the dolphins. Bill Peters was appalled and had the cameraman take footage of the atrocity, but he knew it would never be aired. The whole concept, although strictly legal, was obscene. What Saber didn't count on was Kevin Murphy re-entering the Earth's atmosphere at just the right moment to witness the unsettling event. He had been traveling the far reaches of Earth's solar system, trying to take his mind off the troubling events of the concert. At times he found himself in tears, and at other times strangely removed from all emotion as he recalled the shocking actions of the *humans* in their sexual frenzy. He even wondered if he weren't actually *becoming* something more. It seemed as though the whole of humanity could be reduced to nothing more than a mass of rutting savages if he let his mind travel there for very long. But he was able to return to his normal self for the time being. He was able to care about his brethren, and fortunately, he was able to identify with their finest values.

As Captain Saber was squeezing off shots at the dolphins, the sea began spitting shafts of spray seven feet in the air from the bullets entering the water. Kevin's view-screen increased its magnification from his unconscious mental command, and he saw Saber's shots coming dangerously close to the dolphins. He was furious. He wished he could stop him and the ship was quick to respond. Kevin watched an intense beam of light melt the barrel of the rifle in the captain's hands. Peters heard the captain scream, and then he heard a fierce hissing noise as the beam cut through the deck and the hull as well. At first there were flames surrounding the baseball-sized hole in the deck. Then a blast of steaming hot water shot up through the hole and extinguished the fire. The captain thrust his hands in the air, flapping like a spastic, wounded bird.

A smile appeared on the face of Peters. *What comes around goes around.* Then he alerted the control room at WCIX, "Mayday! Mayday! This is *The Seagull.* We're going down!"

The control room answered, "We read you, Bill. Did you say *The Seagull* is going down?"

"Yes, I think so. We're taking on water faster than the bilge pump can handle it. Is the Coast Guard close enough to respond?" asked Peters.

"Yes, Bill. They're only about ten minutes away. You think you can hold on that long?"

"We'll try. I think the captain is unconscious. We'll get a May West on him in case we have to get in the water."

"Roger, Bill. Good luck to you and your crew."

Before the captain passed out, he was lying on deck screaming in obvious pain. His hands were badly burned, and the blast of light had taken off all the toes on his left foot. Peters put a life jacket around the captain and secured the clasps. After putting one on himself, he and the cameraman, Rodney Ford, held onto the captain as the ship began to slide. When she went under, there was a whirlpool created by the displacement of water.

The Coast Guard had a zodiac in the water and would have them aboard in just a few minutes. Peters and Ford struggled to hang onto the captain until they got there. Saber regained consciousness briefly, and the last thing he saw on that morning was a school of dolphin approaching them as they huddled helplessly in the water. He wished he still had his rifle and two good hands to use it.

When Peters sensed Saber passing out again, he swam up behind him making sure he was in a position to hold the captain's head above the gentle rolling swells of the sea. He was intensely startled a short time later when his feet touched the back of a huge manta ray that came up beneath them. Incredibly, she made no attempt to escape contact with his boat shoes. He almost had the sense that the giant creature was trying to communicate with him in some strange way.

Chapter Twelve
July 12, 2005
3:18 P.M.
Patrick Air Force Base

P atrick Air Force Base is located on a barrier island connected to the eastern coast of Florida by a series of causeways. The causeways span a body of water called the Indian River Lagoon, which is really an estuary more than one hundred fifty-five miles long. It's in the middle of Florida and boasts the title of being the most bio-diverse assembly of life on the planet. Simply put: there are more different species per square mile in the Indian River Lagoon than any other place on Earth. It was one of the reasons that Kevin loved living there. Unfortunately, by a series of accidents in the blink of an eye, he would negatively impact his beloved estuary in a very big way.

On his way ashore from the encounter with *The Seagull,* Kevin wondered for a brief instant what would happen if the island were cut off from the mainland. A brief instant was all it took to remove the question. Three causeways - the Pineda, the Eau Gallie, and the Melbourne Causeway between Sebastian and Canaveral inlets were destroyed by the ship in less than thirty seconds. Miraculously, and partly due to the time of day, there was only one serious injury. A man fishing on the Melbourne

Causeway was thrown into the water when the ship's fantastic speed vaporized the concrete forty yards from where he was standing. He didn't see the ship and told the local police that it must have been a bomb that destroyed the coastal town's artery to the mainland.

One of the seven F-16's that was deployed over the area from Patrick Air Force Base did, however, see the ship. Lt. Franklin Tool made visual contact just as the last of the three causeways went down. He fired two sidewinder missiles that fell harmlessly into the river because they were unable to overtake the alien craft.

"Patrick Tower, this is the Toolman, on Charlie," said Lt. Tool. "Repeat, I'm on Charlie. I have his heading at one-eight-eight degrees, speed roughly Mach-two. I'm falling behind fast."

Whenever military aircraft are over residential areas, they are forbidden to travel faster than the speed of sound. Supersonic speed produces a sonic boom that sometimes shatters windows and knocks paintings off the walls of homes nearby.

"Request permission to light 'em up, Patrick, over."

Lt. Tool's request referred to engaging the F-16's afterburners, which could rapidly increase his airspeed to nearly Mach-3, or two thousand miles per hour.

"Light 'em up, Toolman. Charlie's already broken a few windows."

"Not to mention three causeways! They're history, Patrick! All destroyed. Any intelligence of what we're dealing with, yet?"

"Negative, Toolman. Maintain your heading and hold your ordinance. What is your deployment status?"

"Two sidewinders out. Negative contact. Negative incident."

"Negative incident, well, at least that's something."

"I had a tone for both shots, but he was just too fast. Never seen anything like it, Patrick!"

"Maintain pursuit, Toolman. Beta Squadron should catch you in about three minutes. Delta's heading is two-niner–zero. You should pick them up over Pompano Beach any time now."

"Roger, Patrick."

Kevin Murphy was aware of the fighter jet following behind his craft. The ship was *talking to him* as well as displaying a 360-degree view screen superimposed on the canopy. The screen had the ability to magnify any area of specific focus; however, Kevin wasn't sure exactly how he was conveying the command. The destruction of the causeways was surely a mistake. *A big mistake.* It was entirely unintentional and served as his wake-up call. He would be very careful not to engage any of the fighter aircraft for fear of hurting them.

Kevin's altitude was fourteen hundred feet when he saw the three jets of Delta Squadron coming from the south. He immediately climbed straight up at Mach-five to give himself a little time. His view screen revealed three additional fighters following from the north just in front of the lone fighter he had been leading away from the air force base. They were climbing also and would engage him in about two minutes if he lowered his speed to a sub-sonic level.

He slowed to about four hundred miles per hour and awaited their arrival roughly twenty-six thousand feet above the Atlantic, two miles off the coast of Jensen Beach, Florida. When the fighters came clearly into view without magnification, he slowed his craft to a stop.

"Please don't hurt each other," he prayed aloud. His intention was to let the planes catch him and attempt to destroy his craft. He *knew* this was impossible with the weapons they were carrying, and it would only serve to demonstrate their need to restrain themselves when near a residential area. After all, if they couldn't destroy him, what good would a lot of collateral damage do except enrage the general public?

The fighters first flew at him in crisscross maneuvers coming as close as one hundred feet as they passed. Surprisingly, no missiles were fired. Perhaps they knew that they would be ineffective against a craft that could fly through concrete as easily as it did through the air. What the pilots didn't realize is that the craft didn't blast through the concrete of the causeways at all. Rather, the displacement of the magnetic field was what caused the destruction of the bridges. Magnetic fields hold all matter together. The ship's propulsion system was so powerful that when the sandpaper-like hull came in contact with solid matter it parted instantly to let the ship pass through, much like the way it came ashore beneath the ocean the night before – essentially flying *through* the Earth.

Kevin wasn't entirely sure he was invulnerable to a direct missile strike. He hoped he never had to find out. Maintaining his altitude, he slowly led the fighters out to sea. The skill of the pilots was an impressive display of the American taxpayers' money at work. With each pass, they came closer and closer until Kevin could clearly see their faces. He was relieved when the ship *told him* they weren't able to see his. He knew that cameras were rolling aboard the fighters and the films would be studied intensely in the days ahead to try to determine the origin and intentions of his craft.

Chapter Thirteen
July 12, 2005
5:55 P.M.
Melbourne Beach, Florida

The humid Florida afternoon did little to belay the frenzied anticipation of impending doom all across Brevard County. Something big was happening, and no one was quite sure why the causeways were obliterated. Some surmised that it must have been a meteor shower of some kind. Others thought perhaps the end was near and the wrath of God was raining down on humanity once and for all. Cars were beginning to back up on the causeways. By some stroke of luck, no one had driven off the jagged edges of the mammoth structures before the local police were able to set up barricades. The police cars, however, would remain stranded at the top of the causeways for some time. A steady flow of cars was packing the roadway before they could be diverted back to the barrier island.

At Patrick Air Force Base, Kevin's craft was hovering three feet over the middle of runway one-eight-zero. He had led the fighters three hundred miles off the coast and then returned to shore in only twenty seconds. He was amazed that the gravitational forces of his fantastic acceleration hadn't squashed him like a bug. All he felt was a gentle pressure settling him into his seat. What was even more amazing was the fact that Kevin's craft traveled so fast that it was literally undetectable by the radar array surrounding the air force base.

"What the..?" said air traffic controller, Sgt. Ed Blue. He seemed to see the alien craft instantly appear out of thin air.

"Excuse me, Sergeant?" asked Captain Bob Ellis still not aware of what had captured his subordinate airman's attention. He turned away from the radar screen monitoring the fighters out at sea and looked out the window toward the ship on the runway. Ellis felt his knees weaken slightly as he reached for the support of the desk beside him. He never took his eyes off the ship as he said, "Call the general, Ed."

Sergeant Blue punched in the numbers for General Steven Hightower's command center and handed the phone to Captain Ellis.

"General, this is Captain Ellis at approach control. We have a bogey on one-eight-zero, and I believe it's Charlie."

"Are you trying to tell me that there's a space ship on your runway, Bobby?" The General was trying to cut through the tension that they both were feeling. He knew the value of an alert and clear thinking staff at a time such as this.

"Affirmative, Sir."

"Just keep your eye on it, Captain," said the general. He motioned to his driver, Sergeant Jim Sherman, by silently raising his eyebrows and turning his head toward the door. The sergeant left instantly to retrieve his jeep and have it running just outside the command center door when the general emerged.

"Orders, Sir?" said his second in command, Colonel Cliff Byrd.

"Cliff, I want twenty airmen surrounding that ship in sixty seconds," said the general rubbing his palms down his face. It had been a long day and it was far from over yet.

"M-16's, General?"

"No weapons, Cliff. That's a direct order. Make sure they get it right. Twenty airmen standing at attention, that's all."

"Yes, Sir," said Colonel Byrd.

General Hightower knew he shouldn't even be thinking what he was about to do next. He had spent the last thirty-four years of his life in the air force. He had a good life and a successful career. *This is as good a time as any - to meet my maker.* The general exuded confidence and it was infectious. He exuded bravery, and it was contagious. Above all, the general was a fair man. It was widely known that he never asked a man to do something he hadn't done or wouldn't do himself. Colonel Byrd didn't ask, but he was well aware of what the general's next move would be.

As he left the room and headed toward the elevator, the general lit a fat cigar. He flicked an ash at the "no smoking" sign when he stepped inside. He pressed the button for the ground floor and held up his hand to stop the colonel from shadowing his movements. "Not this time, Cliff. You're the only one who can run the show. Don't worry, I'll be all right. Back in twenty minutes."

"Yes, Sir," said the colonel with a show of concern clearly on his face. The elevator doors closed on a cloud of smoke.

~

July 12, 2005
6:07 P.M.
Patrick Air Force Base
Runway One-Eight-Zero

The airmen stood in a perfect circle around the ship. Fear was evident on their faces, but the moment was broken when the general walked through the circle directly up to the ship and rapped his knuckles on the hull. All the men were silent, and they had to hold themselves back from laughing as the general said, "Hello. Is anybody home? You've just cost the American taxpayers a lot of money. What have you got to say for yourself?" The craft stood deathly silent. The general then continued, "Come on, show yourself."

Kevin Murphy was resting quietly inside the ship. He had dozed off for a short while, just a ten-minute catnap. He vaguely remembered dreaming about his dog, Misty. He'd dreamt that she'd run away from home. He was awakened by a dull rapping on the hull of the ship. He opened his laptop computer and booted up the electronic voice response program.

"How do you explain the destruction of our roadways? Is this your attempt at peaceful communication with our species?" asked the general.

Kevin typed his reply on the laptop's keyboard, and then he hit the return button, *"IT WAS A MISTAKE,"* came the electronically generated voice from inside the ship.

The sound produced was amplified to almost one-hundred-fifty decibels and boomed across the tarmac. When he noticed the reaction of the general and the startled airmen, he turned the volume down. He then typed, *"Can you hear me, General?"*

"We can hear you," responded Hightower. The sound from the ship was only half as loud as the first time, and the general realized that whoever was inside the ship had turned it down. This was encouraging because it meant that the visitor was not infallible. He was working the bugs out of this encounter just as they were.

"How is it that you know our language?" asked the general.

"We know all your languages," replied the ship. *"We have been watching you for some time now,"* bluffed Kevin.

"Where do you come from?" asked the general.

"*Well beyond your solar system,*" replied Kevin cryptically. He was starting to enjoy his little exchange with the general.

"Could you be a little more specific? asked General Hightower.

"*A planet revolving the star you call Sirius. It's in the constellation of Orion,*" replied Kevin.

"You're a student of astronomy," stated the general.

A mental alarm went off in Kevin's head. *Be careful, Kevin. Don't tip your hand.* He thought he might have said too much already, but he couldn't help himself. He was having too much fun.

"*We are students of many things as well as your astronomy. We are also students of your aggression toward each other. We find this characteristic . . . disturbing.*"

"Is that so? Well, so do we. However, we also find it . . . necessary," taunted Hightower. Something told him that he wasn't dealing with an intelligent being from another world. He wasn't exactly sure what it was, perhaps just an instinct. But instincts were generally accurate for him in the past, and he felt he could bet all three of his stars on this one.

"*You are the only creatures on your planet to engage in violence,*" typed Kevin.

"Some of our animals are very violent. I invite you to find out. Just invite a leopard into your ship there, or maybe a Bengal tiger," said the general.

"Survival instincts are not violent. In fact, we know that predators feel much compassion for their prey. We are surprised that you have no knowledge of this," said the mechanical voice.

The general decided to try another tactic, "Tell me. Since you know our languages, why don't you speak in your real voice? Why do you use the machine?" asked the general.

"We lack the ability to generate sound waves from our bodies as you do," was the reply.

"How do you communicate among your own species?"

"We have no need to do so. We share the same thoughts."

"The same thoughts," parroted the general. "That's very good." He knew it was just a matter of time before the ship's occupant or occupants made a mistake. He just wanted to keep him talking. *Let his own ego be his undoing,* thought the general. "So what now?" he asked.

"The violence shall end," typed Kevin from inside the ship.

"Sounds like you want to put me out of a job."

Chapter Fourteen
July 12, 2005
6:15 P.M.
Sebastian Inlet

Misty was lying on the dunes by the south jetty at Sebastian Inlet. She had traveled almost fifteen miles south of her former home. Normally, it would take her no more than three hours of mindless, though determined, trotting to get there. But she took her time since July 9th, sleeping under the dune crossovers and searching for something ripe from the sea she could either eat or roll in. Her usual frantic dashes to stir up the seagulls and sandpipers were set aside. If someone didn't know that the power of reason was beyond the capacity of animals, he might think that the dog had something on her mind.

The jetty was packed with fishermen. One of them was using a brand new Penn 750 reel that he had just bought with his poker winnings from Kevin Murphy's house. Mike was after a snook. The illusive game fish usually promised good sport during an outgoing tide. Mike was reeling in after being "cleaned" when he glanced down the jetty to the south dunes. *Is that Misty?* He called to her, "Here, Misty. Here, girl." The dog didn't respond. *Sure looks like her. Nah, it couldn't be.* There was no sign of Kevin. Mike went back to his snook fishing. If Misty heard Mike calling, she certainly didn't show it. It seemed as if she had forgotten her name.

~

July 12, 2005
6:25 P.M.
Patrick Air Force Base
Runway One-Eight-Zero

The general sensed his encounter coming to an end and was desperate to keep the conversation going.

"We, as Americans, want the violence to end, also. Our desire is for a world at peace; however, there are certain religious factions who are against us and challenge us with threats to our well being. It is not safe for Americans to travel outside our country. Therefore, we have agreed with other nations to undermine the actions of the terrorists," continued the general.

"Thereby killing innocent civilians in countries weaker than yourself."

"There is collateral damage, yes. But that is not our intent. We target only the military of the countries that support terrorism."

"Perhaps the innocent civilians consider the Americans terrorists," typed Kevin.

"I'm sure they do," said the general. "But we hit them by accident. They intentionally target our civilians."

"It is our belief that the intention is immaterial when death is the result. Death is death. It is against the will of creation. Therefore, the violence shall end."

"That sounds like a threat," said the general.

"It is merely a prediction."

"And your species has no problem interfering with the development of civilizations more primitive than your own?" asked the general angrily.

"We are glad to help," said the ship.

"What is it you plan to do?" asked the general.

"We have a device which can destabilize the magnetic field of any object, even from a great distance. It essentially reduces inorganic matter to dust. It does not, however, cause any harm to living things. Shall I demonstrate on one of your fighter planes that are just now returning from out at sea?"

The general could hear the screaming of the powerful jet engines overhead as the words were spoken.

"That won't be necessary," said the general.

"Then order them to stand down, General. All of your fighters shall return to your base immediately."

"What then? Do you plan to meet with world leaders to propose your plan for peace?"

"That won't be necessary," said Kevin from the ship.

"What do you mean?" asked the general.

"We are planning a demonstration of our depolarization capability from your satellite two-hundred-forty thousand miles away."

"You mean the moon."

"Yes."

"What do you intend to depolarize?"

"Your largest battleship."

"Whoa now, wait a minute. I don't think that will be necessary," said the general. "I think that we can negotiate a peace without a demonstration."

"It must be a peace both in action and intent. If we discover any deception on your part, the demonstration will be forthcoming."

"I understand. Give me some time to inform our leader of your intentions."

"You have three days," said the ominous voice from the ship.

"That isn't very much time," said the general.

"Arrange for one of your battleships that is no longer in service to be towed ten miles off your coast. Aim your most powerful telescope at the moon. We shall inscribe the name of the ship on the surface of the moon, and then we shall depolarize it."

"I'm not sure I can arrange that," said the general.

"We feel that it is an equitable alternative to destabilizing your largest battleship."

"I get your point," said the general wearily.

Chapter Fifteen
July 12, 2005
9:55 P.M.
West Melbourne, Florida

Kevin had had enough for one day. He figured it was time to put the ship to bed. He had learned a great deal about the many elaborate systems aboard the ship. There was, in fact, an advanced weapons system despite Kevin's lie about the depolarization device. The main weapon was a programmed series of electromagnetic radiation pulses, not unlike a laser. The major difference being the pulses from Kevin's ship were incredibly silent. He was confident that they could produce a devastating force to the surface of the Earth all the way from the surface of the moon.

Kevin reached the pasture where his pick-up was parked just after the sun had finished casting its afterglow across the horizon. It was finally dark enough to risk a descent to Earth unnoticed. Just to be on the safe side, he rose to a hundred thousand feet and located the pasture with the help of the magnification screen. Then he fell straight down to evade any radar detection. He felt he was finally getting the hang of it. When he slid his body forward, the canopy opened as the ship had *told* him it would. He slid down the side of the ship and removed the stone from its cradle. As soon as he had it in his hand, the canopy began to close up again. It was very warm to the touch. He decided to remove the stone from the starboard side of the ship as well, but when he rounded the stern, he could see that the cradle was empty. His curiosity reached out to the ship for an answer regarding the stone's absence, but for some reason it didn't have anything to say about the matter.

Then he pressed the forward icon of the stone he was holding and moved the ship over a large grassy lake by the side of the pasture. He pointed the stone down and the ship went under. When he felt the rumbling of the Earth beneath him, he pressed the reverse icon to stop the ship's forward progress.

He dug a small hole near the base of an old oak tree and placed the stone there. When the hole was filled and the ground was covered with leaves and palm fronds, he felt confident enough to leave his terrible treasure behind. Kevin's old Ford pick-up truck welcomed him back to the realm of humanity. For the first time in what seemed like a lifetime, he understood the luxury he enjoyed as Kevin Murphy able to merely slip into the crowd, neither noticed nor noteworthy. He drove to the new Front-Street Marina in Melbourne and parked his truck in one of the double-length trailer spaces.

His trip to the mainland earlier had taken over an hour and a half. He had to travel south to state road 510, the Wabasso Causeway, and then cross over to 1 US. If he left his truck on the mainland, the boat trip would only be a fraction of the time. He retrieved his bicycle from the back of the truck and bought a ride on a platform boat back to the barrier-island. The rate had gone down dramatically as more boats responded to the area to assist the island residents. He only paid twelve dollars for the fifteen-minute ride. When he reached the Indialantic Fishing Pier, which was being used as an emergency embarkation point to the mainland, he rode his bicycle across the pier and down Riverside Drive to his home in Melbourne Beach.

He arrived home a short time later and saw two messages blinking on his answering machine. He pressed the recall button, *"Kevin, it's Brenda. Call me, will you. Tell me what's going on up there. Ronald-The-Great is pooping his pants. Thanks, bye,"* said the message. He had no intention of responding to that message. The second one said, "Hi, Kevin, it's your mother. Call me as soon as you get this message. Your father had another coronary."

Kevin quickly dialed his mother's cell phone.

"Hello," said his mother.

"Mom! How's Dad?" said Kevin nervously.

"He's okay for now. The doctor said the worst is over. Thank God, I had his pills with me. I keep them in my golf bag."

"You were on the golf course?"

"Yes. The third hole, second shot. Your father finally hit that green from over the water when this piercing noise cut across the sky. We turned around and saw the Air

Force plane chasing that awful thing from off the coast. He grabbed his chest, and I knew he was having another one. We had to go to Wuestoff. Holmes was out of the question according to the EMT's. They said the causeways had been blown up. It must be terrorism, but I'm trying not to alarm your father. When can you get to the hospital? He's out of ICU and back to a room now."

"I don't have my truck, Mom."

"You don't? Where is it?"

"It's a long story. Can you pick me up?"

"I guess so. I'm supposed to be going back to your father right now. I just stopped home to get some of his things."

"You go on ahead, Mom. I'll get a ride with someone else."

"Are you sure?"

"Yeah, I'm sure. What room is he in?"

"Three-ten."

"Okay. I'll see you when I get there."

"All right, Sweetie. And don't worry. Your father's a pretty tough man."

"You're pretty tough yourself, Mom."

Chapter Sixteen
July 12, 2005
10:53 P.M.
Rockledge, Florida

Kevin walked through the front entrance of Wuestoff Medical Center and went to the visitor's desk for a pass.

"My name is Kevin Murphy. My father is in room three-ten. Do I need a pass?"

"No, Mr. Murphy. You can go right up. Take the second elevator bank on your left," she said pointing, "down that hallway. Just follow the green line."

"Thank you," he said as he headed off to the elevator.

When he reached the room, he was startled to see his father with an I-V in his arm and an oxygen mask connected to a tube, which disappeared into the wall behind his bed. His mother rose from a chair and greeted him, "Hi, Kevin. What took you so long?"

"I had to borrow Susan's car. It took me about twenty minutes to track her down."

"Didn't she come with you?"

"No, Mom. She had to work."

"Uh huh," said his mother. "Some girlfriend."

"She's volunteering in a clinic set up over at the Methodist Church. Panic counseling, Mom. She takes her job pretty seriously."

"Well, your father is pretty serious, too. One of these times he's not going to make it."

"I'm so sorry, Mom. Is there anything I can do?"

"Just be here, Honey. When your father wakes up he'll be glad to see you."

~

July 12, 2005
11:18 P.M.
Sebastian Inlet

Mike was loading up his gear into his pickup at Sebastian Inlet when he saw the dog again. *Ranger's gonna' pick her up soon.* He tried again, "Misty? Is that you?"

The dog trotted over to his side and sat down.

"What a good girl you are. But what are you doing here? Where's Kevin, Misty." The dog had no reaction for him.

"How 'bout I take you home, Sweetie."

The dog then darted away toward the beach.

"Misty, come back here," shouted Mike, but the dog never turned around. *That's strange.* Mike got into his truck and headed home. On his way back he dialed Kevin's cell phone. Kevin picked up on the third ring, "Hello."

"Kevin. It's Mike."

"Hey, man. What's up?"

"Sorry for the late call. I think I just saw your dog."

"Misty? Where'd you see her?" asked Kevin. "Are you in Melbourne Beach?"

"I'm down at the inlet. Been tryin' to get a snook. She's been around here all night," said Mike.

"So how come you didn't pick her up?"

"She wouldn't come to me. She bolted."

"That's not Misty," said Kevin. "There's more than one English Pointer around here."

"Where're you now," asked Mike.

"I'm at Wuesthoff. My dad's had another heart attack."

"Man. That's rough," said Mike. "Let me know if there's anything I can do."

"Thanks, buddy. I will." Kevin hung up his phone.

"Who was that?"

"That was Mike, Mom. He said he . . ."

"Kevin? Is that you?" he heard a weak voice from the bed.

"Dad!" said Kevin. "How're you doin' Buddy?"

"I'm all right."

"Well, you don't look all right. You better lay off golf for a week or two," said Kevin fighting back tears.

"I just got startled that's all. Damn ticker isn't what she used to be," he said.

"I'm sure you'll be fine in a few days," said Kevin. "Just rest, Dad."

"I intend to," he said. "Might read a book for a change."

"That'd be good, Dad. How would you like the new Michael Crichton novel?"

"Whatever."

"Just rest, Dad. I'm gonna go get the book now. Can I bring you anything else?"

"Not really. Just the book."

"I love you, Dad."

"I love you, too, Son."

Chapter Seventeen
July 13, 2005
1:06 A.M.
Satellite Beach, Florida

On his way back home to Melbourne Beach, Kevin stopped in Satellite Beach to return Susan's car and retrieve his bicycle. Susan was still at the Emergency Panic Management Clinic set up in the Methodist Church on Jackson Avenue. He wanted to give her back her keys and talk about his father's condition.

Despite the late hour, the clinic was crowded with very agitated people. They ranged from merely shaking to preaching end-of-the-world predictions resulting from the havoc reeked by the strange craft that Kevin had tucked away in West Melbourne. Kevin asked the triage nurse where Susan was working with her group. She directed him to one of the Sunday school classrooms along the eastern side of the building. He walked his bicycle to room 12. Looking through the window, his eyes locked with Susan's, and he detected frostiness in her demeanor. She opened the door and briefly spoke to him in an urgent hushed tone, "This is not a good time, Kevin."

"What? Am I interrupting you and the good doctor or something?" asked Kevin barely concealing an animosity that surprised him. It had been festering just beneath the surface of his conscious mind, slippery and fleeting when he tried to focus on it. *She betrayed me,* he thought to himself. *How could've I forgotten that? What the hell's wrong with me?* he wondered.

Kevin noticed a tear welling up in her eye and it dismantled his fury. He wasn't quite sure what he witnessed at the Dave Matthews concert, but he had a bad feeling about it all the same.

"What is it, Sue?" he inquired of her tearful display.

Susan stepped outside the meeting room and closed the door quickly behind her. She wiped her eyes with the back of her hand and said, "Kevin, I'm quitting. This is my last day."

"I just stopped by to thank you for the . . ."

"He raped me," she hissed in a forced whisper.

"What are you talking about, Sue."

"Doc Singer. At least I think he did – I don't know, I'm so confused. Just leave me, please. It's not a good time."

"What do you mean he raped you?" asked Kevin knowing all too well what she was alluding to. The image came back to him – trying to burn itself in his mind. Still he couldn't quite focus on the memory. He knew that the ship was affecting him somehow. It worried him that the side effects of exposure to the alien craft could be something serious like Alzheimer's or pre-senile dementia, but he couldn't focus there for very long either. He seemed to be developing some sort of adult A.D.D.

"It might have been DMSO," said Susan.

"What?" asked Kevin.

"Roofies in a squirt gun."

"Listen to yourself, Sue. I don't think you're firing on all cylinders, Doctor Lang."

"Look, it was a concert, okay? Lots of wacko people there just like every concert. I think that I was squirted with a drug that was suspended in a saturation medium called DMSO. It makes you absorb the drug through the skin."

"What drug?" asked Kevin.

"Ruphenhol, the date rape drug," said Susan.

"I think you're being a little paranoid, Sue."

"Kevin, I woke up from a seizure with my shirt off and I felt like I had just been . . . violated," she said finally – tears once again filling her eyes."

"Jesus," said Kevin. "Are you sure?"

"No, I'm not, but I know I can't work here any longer."

"I don't blame you. You think that Doc Singer squirted you with the drug?"

"I don't know what I think. He was pretty upset, too, when it happened. We didn't even stay for the concert."

"Where did you go?" he asked her.

"To the hospital in Tampa. Singer said he didn't trust himself to drive."

"Jesus," said Kevin again. "Maybe you both got squirted."

"What is wrong with people, Kevin? How could someone do that?"

"Hell if I know," he said. "Can't you just put it behind you?"

"Maybe," she said. "But that's not all of it."

"What do you mean?" he asked her.

"She *called me,* Kevin," said Susan miserably.

"What?"

"Your Ex."

"Oh, God. I'm so sorry, Sue."

"Yeah, well, me too. Look, Kevin, there's just too much going on right now for me to sort it all out. I'll be home for breakfast, and maybe we can talk then, okay?"

"Okay," was all he could think to say. Susan opened the door and went back inside to her group. Kevin just stood there looking at the concrete for a moment. "Damn it, Brenda," he cried looking up at the sky. "What do you want from me? You made your bed, now try lying in it," he said referring to her choice to leave him for a man who made more money. He got back on his bicycle and started down Jackson Street to A-1-A.

A-1-A is largely a four-lane highway that runs along the East Coast of Florida. His little town of Melbourne Beach is one of the few places where it narrows down to only two. That was part of the appeal for Kevin when he and Brenda decided to purchase a house. Ironically, she now lives in an area where there is considerably more traffic. Kevin thought it served her right.

It has always been his observation that people generally get what they deserve. If someone is truly a small town person, they protect their town from expansion. Unfortunately, many people aren't honest enough about their true natures. They endear themselves to the community only to gain a footing and knowledge necessary to exploit it. It's the same song over and over in the sad state that Florida finds herself in today.

The traffic was unusually light along the highway. He imagined that many people were making the trip across the river to the Melbourne area or possibly out of town. It was almost comical to think that a ship could travel light-years to Earth, and people thought they could protect themselves by putting a few-hundred or even a thousand miles behind them. One thing was clear. The general public was harboring unnecessary senseless fear that was not alleviated by the powers that be. Kevin's intention was to demonstrate that the general public was in no danger from the craft, despite the obvious mistake involving the causeways. He hoped that the Air Force base would inform the public that they were in contact with the aliens and quell their fears. For some reason that satisfaction was not a part of the military's agenda. Again, Kevin had a lot to think about.

Susan came in at five-thirty in the morning after seventeen straight hours at the clinic. She skipped breakfast and went straight to bed. When Kevin woke her at two in the afternoon, he apologized with breakfast in bed as well as a generous helping of affection.

"I want to be with you, Kevin, but I'm not sure you're worth the trouble," said Susan.

"Yes, you are," he said nibbling on her earlobe.

"If you weren't so charming, buster, you'd be out on the street right now," she said teasingly.

"But it's my house," he said in his defense.

Chapter Eighteen
July 13, 2005
7:15 P.M.
Vero Beach, Florida

Brenda's house was a block west of A-1-A in Vero Beach. It was only a short distance away from a popular French restaurant called Chez Henri. Kevin and Brenda had had many dinners there celebrating special occasions. He knew the layout of the restaurant intimately and was ruminating about the central dining room that had a fireplace behind glass doors as well as an antique chandelier that was the focal point of the room. It was huge. Over four hundred crystal prisms reflected light from every source imaginable. It was a true work of art that was originally designed with gas florets, which were converted to electricity some sixty years ago. It hung over a circular table that could seat a dozen people.

Kevin imagined Brenda eating dinner there and was anxious to vent his anger at her for calling Susan. *The nerve of her!* Susan was a sweet girl who had nothing to do with Brenda. Harassing her was surely only a dig at Kevin for some reason beyond his comprehension. *What could she want? She had her precious money. She held out on old Ronny until he would marry her. So what's the deal?*

Kevin decided he'd better put a stop to her atrocious behavior. He dialed her from his cell phone, "Brenda."

"Kevin. So you finally got my message. What's going . . .?"

"Listen, Brenda. I'm not sure what you want from me, but leave Susan out if it, okay?"

"Stop worrying about your precious Susan," she snipped.

"Don't get on my bad side, Brenda. You'll be sorry."

"Ooh, I'm so scared of the big bad trim carpenter," she chided.

"Brenda, you are one sorry piece of work, you know that? I've done nothing to you. Why are you hassling me?" asked Kevin.

"I'm not trying to do anything, Kevin. I'm just scared. Ron is living at the bottom of a bottle right now. He can't even drive. If I have to leave here, I'm going to leave him where he is. Maybe I'll leave forever. Is it too late for us?"

"You *know* it is, Brenda. Please don't call Susan again. Could you do that for me?"

"Yes, Kevin. I'm sorry. I was just . . . you know, lonely."

"I'm sorry, Bren. I can't help you now."

"I know."

"You at Chez Henri?"

"Yeah."

"How's the Dover sole?"

"Not so good."

"Yeah, well, nothing lasts forever."

"I still love you, Kevin."

"Good bye, Brenda. Take care of yourself."

"Someone has to."

~

Susan walked into the room just as Kevin was hanging up the phone. She asked him, "Is it over?"

"Oh, Sue. It's *so* over," said Kevin.

"Then why did she call?" asked Susan.

"She's scared I guess," said Kevin.

"Well, who's not," said Susan. "Everybody's scared."

"We'll be all right, Sue. I promise."

"As long as you only promise me, Kevin."

"Done."

Kevin and Susan went for a walk on the beach to look for Misty. She'd never been gone for three days since she'd started her nasty habit of digging out of the yard, but Kevin wasn't particularly worried. He thought that perhaps it was a residual effect from contact with the ship. He felt as if he would *know* if anything bad had happened to his dog. He didn't know why, but he didn't question it either. Misty had run away before and always came back unscathed. Kevin and Susan held hands just as they had done when they first dated. Kevin looked in her eyes and said, "I love you, Sue."

"I know," she said.

"That's it?" he asked.

"That's it."

He didn't press the issue any further. Brenda calling her had taken its toll. He knew it would be some time before the tension would subside completely. Susan was worth the wait.

He wondered exactly what Brenda said to her, but his instincts told him to drop it for now. Maybe they could talk about it over an anniversary toast. *After all, he couldn't be held responsible for her behavior, right? Poor, Brenda. Poor, rich, Brenda.*

Chapter Nineteen
July 13, 2005
8:15 P.M.
Melbourne Beach, Florida

Kevin and Susan were walking on the beach a short distance from their house on Third Avenue. He felt the great weight of his terrible secret. He wanted to let Susan in on it. He needed a partner to keep him in check. She was a sober thinker, and he loved her, trusted her, and respected her values as much as his own. But how could he be sure she would understand the mistakes he made? The causeways were a catastrophe. Thousands of lives were in the balance. He may have even killed his own father. Maybe if he had been able to reach the medical center in Melbourne instead of Rockledge, there would have been less damage to his heart. There was so much to think about, and he couldn't afford any more mistakes. He asked her, "What if you could control that ship that's caused all the commotion, Sue? What would you do?"

"What?" she asked.

"The space ship. What if you could control it?"

"I'd send it away, Kevin."

"You're kidding?" he asked.

"No, I'm not. Look what's it's done so far. It'll be years until we're back to normal here on the island."

"But that was a mistake, Sue. What if you could do good things with it?"

"A mistake?" she asked. "How do you know that?"

"The ship is in communication with the Air Force Base. It said there was no intention to destroy the causeways. It just flew through them by mistake."

"How do you know that, Kevin? I haven't heard anything about the Air Force Base talking to them."

"My dad told me," he lied.

"How's he doing?"

"Not so good. This one was worse than the last one."

"I'm sorry, Kevin. Can I help in some way?"

"I don't think so."

Kevin was all too aware of the fact that there were two seats in the craft. He felt it was predestined that he would share his find with Susan, but how could he broach the subject. *Oh, by the way, I destroyed the causeways.* He was conflicted in a way that he had never imagined he could be. It was such a pregnant moment. A wonderful secret laced with endless possibilities. He was bursting with a desire to share it with someone. Perhaps if she had told him that she loved, him the decision would have been easier for him. He decided to wait for the time being.

There was a tropical storm forming out in the Atlantic that the National Weather Service was beginning to watch. The designated name was Freda with sustained winds of forty miles per hour. She was still several days away from threatening any landmasses, but in the wake of

Hurricane Andrew, memories were still recovering from a wariness of potential nightmares. Florida had been lucky since Andrew. She enjoyed ten years of relatively mild hurricane activity. Her luck wouldn't last forever.

The shuttle fleet had just begun flying again after the Columbia disaster in January. Atlantis was on a mission to Alpha, the International Space Station, and was due to land at Kennedy in six days. That gave Freda somewhat more attention than any ordinary tropical storm. A diversion to Edwards Air Force Base by a shuttle meant an additional million dollars of the taxpayer's money. Atlantis was the first shuttle to fly since Columbia, and everyone knew there would be no gambling on chances for safe landing. Any storm brewing in the Atlantic meant that Edwards would get the landing.

The next few days were a series of highs and lows as the stock markets plummeted and there began a cessation of all hostile activity by warring nations throughout the world. There were no suicide bombers in Israel, no bombings in Northern Ireland, no border conflicts between India and Pakistan, and no anti-aircraft fire from Iraq over the no fly zone. The world was strangely quiet. Waiting. Watching the skies. Bouncing grandchildren on their knees.

Susan was spending less time at the clinic and had begun considering the normal resumption of her practice. Her patients had been very understanding and generous in sharing her with the clinic. It seemed that people who dealt with conflict on a daily basis were much more capable of handling the stress of a new situation. It was business as usual for many of the emotionally challenged people who Susan worked with. She was proud of their strength and was eager to recognize them for it. They deserved it. She would be surprised to learn that many of her patients were a source of strength for the quote, "*normal people*" of the community during the crisis involving the unknown craft.

Chapter Twenty
July 14, 2005
10:40 P.M.
Melbourne Beach, Florida

There had been no sign of the craft since July 12th, and many people were becoming restless. No news was bad news. The Navy had complied with the instructions that the aliens gave for their demonstration. They were to show the world, during an orchestrated attack on a U.S. Navy vessel, that they had the ability to destroy military machines in an instant from the surface of the moon. This would drive home the point that there was no hiding from their retribution should the people of Earth fail to heed their call for peace. They had towed the *U.S.S. Valiant*, a heavy cruiser, ten miles offshore from the mothball fleet in Norfolk, Virginia. She displaced one-hundred-forty-thousand tons, which made for a laborious venture in that her power plant had long since been removed during her retirement. Four tugboats completed the task in a little over two days. During that time, the world was experiencing mixed emotions regarding the upcoming demonstration. Everyone was anxious to see the terrible force that the ship could unleash, and yet they were well aware of the ghastly implications. The world could be thrust into the position of unconditional surrender to a single alien spacecraft.

~

July 14, 2005
10:44 PM
Mauna Kea Summit, Hawaii

A graduate student from the University of Hawaii was the first to spot the name of the battleship inscribed on the moon. Painstakingly working a grid of the moon's surface, students from the University's School of Astronomical Studies programmed the huge reflective lens atop the Mauna Kea Summit to focus on areas as small as ten thousand square feet. Mauna Kea is nearly fourteen thousand feet above sea level and is the home of the largest concentration of telescopes in the world. It stands above ninety-eight percent of the Earth's atmosphere and affords an unparalleled view of the heavens.

The students took forty-minute shifts monitoring video screens and manning the eyepiece as the telescope's huge motors slowly moved the focal point across the grid. The excited young co-ed named Sidney Peel shouted, "There it is! It says, *U.S.S. Valiant.!*"

The shapely grad student gained instant fame by what would be called, *"Peel's Observation at Mauna Kea, 10:44 PM on July 14th, 2005."*

Kevin Murphy was anxious to get the demonstration behind him. He was leery of using the craft's awesome force against a point on the Earth's surface. What if he blasted a hole to the Earth's core? He wasn't positive he could control the ship's great power. The shot on the shrimp boat scuttled her, and he injured Saber pretty badly, but the bolt of light hadn't gone much further than *The Seagull's* lower planking. It was as if the ship *knew* his intention and carried out an action with the necessary force. Would the ship know how much force was necessary to scuttle the cruiser and not pierce the Earth itself? He could only hope so. All his instincts told him that it could.

It was not a malevolent thing. It was merely a tool to be used for positive or negative action. Mankind was malevolent as demonstrated by centuries of conflict. He was becoming intolerant of his own species. The ship was changing him in ways that were just below his consciousness.

He had always been a pacifist, but now his pacifism bore an urgency that bordered on violence. He was becoming more conflicted every time he entered the ship. He was also prepared to take more chances. The last time he put the ship under the lake, he brought the control stone back home with him. He was prepared to bring the ship to him when he needed it and risk discovery.

Perhaps a part of him wanted to be discovered - maybe even wanted to force a confrontation. He told himself that wasn't the case, but the ship was telling him things, also. One of the things it told him was that he wasn't the first person to discover and use the great ship. On his second manned flight when he wrote the name of the *U.S.S. Valiant* on The Sea of Tranquility, he discovered an artifact from the last of the ship's prior pilots.

On the floor of the ship between the starboard-side seat and the control-stone console, he saw a small object. It was a braided piece of leather with a small pouch at one end and a tiny egret's feather on the other. As soon as he picked it up, his mind began to fill with images of a dark-skinned man who was known as Coal-Eyed Joe.

He *knew* then that the small pouch was filled with a white powdery aphrodisiac made from the crushed antlers of the Florida Key deer. The feather was a symbol of fertility passed down from the elders of the Miccosukee Indian tribe. They believed that the Gods landed in a lake in northern Florida near Tallahassee and swam ashore. The legend stated that just prior to the landing of the Gods, the tribe was stirred to a frenzy to *"bring fourth the young ones,"* in a field known as, *"the place of the white bird."* From that time on, the egret feather was known to help the members of the tribe do the will of the Gods by procreating. Some claim that the feather is still used to this day in foreplay by the Miccosukee elders when teaching the young Indians the, *"secrets of the body."*

The images gave Kevin some comfort because he knew that Coal-Eyed-Joe had used the ship some one-hundred-seventy-eight years before him. He wondered what happened to the young Indian and was *given* the answer in a series of pictures and sounds that filled his mind as though he was sitting in a stadium-like seat of a cinematic theatre.

Coal-Eyed Joe was awakened one morning by his woman, Cesta Luna, whose name meant *Light from the Moon*. She asked him to dig for oysters on a rocky shoal of the east side of the Halifax River. He paddled his cypress dugout canoe to the rich bed just before the sun would climb eagerly over the eastern horizon.

The mouth of the river was only an arrow's flight distance from the New Smyrna inlet where the outgoing tide would expose the oyster beds to a few lucky terns and seagulls. For about thirty minutes, twice a day, at the ebb of a fast moving tide, the rich oyster bed was fairly easy to harvest. The fact that low tide occurred so early one day would change his life forevermore.

Kevin reached out with his mind into the life of the small black tribesman to the day when he discovered the strange blue stone lodged mysteriously into the oyster bed. It lay there so long that the mollusks decided to grow obliviously around it until it was nearly out of sight. But the young Indian caught site of the strange blue light just as the tide had uncovered the bed shortly before the sunrise. It wasn't bright enough to be noticed during the harsh daylight, but before dawn, the Indian caught sight of the strange stone glowing with a light of its own.

He was left with no choice but to dig it out of the bed and examine it. *Such a treasure,* he thought to himself, *I will make a necklace for Cesta Luna. Then she will surely ask me to bring her a fresh feather from the small white bird. Our family will grow to a great size with many fields of corn to manage.*

When Coal-Eyed Joe's hand first touched the stone, his thoughts turned immediately to Cesta Luna. He thought of how the sun was such a bright spot on her hair, smoother and darker than the wing of a raven. He thought of her shape and the swell of her breast since they were once young together. He liked the changes, suddenly now more than ever. And he thought of her hips beckoning him to lay with him on the soft deer skins.

When he lifted the stone free from the oyster bed, a great round rock burst forth from the sea like the breaching of an angry whale. So startled was Coal-Eyed Joe that he dropped the stone. The great rock then disappeared beneath the waves. He squatted there for a full five minutes watching the area of the ocean where the strange rock went down. He no longer thought of Cesta Luna or any other woman. He couldn't tear his mind from the magical appearance of the great rock from the sea. When his heartbeat slowed to nearly its normal pace again, he took his gaze from the ocean and looked back down to where he had dropped the stone. He noticed again its color and also came to the realization that the strange rock from the sea was also that color. They were both the color of the sky. He reached down and again picked up the blue stone.

Instantly the great rock from the ocean broke the surface of the waves. This time, Coal-Eyed Joe did not drop the stone. Instead, he looked at it more closely and compared it to the color of the rock from the sea. He saw that they were the same. He raised the stone up over his head and was amazed to see that the great blue rock rose, also. Then he lowered the stone back down and saw that the great rock followed the motion of his hand. It was then that he began to understand the enormity of his discovery. "This is not to be a necklace for Cesta Luna," he declared out loud. "This, the Gods have sent to me that I may do their will. Finally he dared to add, "This shall some day soon make me one of them."

It was then that Coal-Eyed Joe noticed something strange about the fish. They were all trying to gather together beneath the strange blue rock. The sea seemed to boil with whitecaps in the area just below the otherworldly craft; he was now sure that he understood its true purpose. It was a tool just as his cypress dugout was a tool – nothing more or less. The only difference was the length of the river it may be able to traverse. Coal-Eyed Joe even thought he heard the sound of a whale.

Kevin was instantly transported forward to an incident back in 1827, known as The Massacre at Indian Key. Ninety-seven white men, women and children were brutally massacred by the Miccosukee Black Indians in retaliation for what was thought to be an artillery attack from a ship off the Florida coast. It was a ship indeed; however, it sailed the sky instead of the seas.

Coal-Eyed Joe was looking through the view screen when he had finally boarded the ship, which enabled him to see an impossible distance. He since had learned that the ship was able to make itself unseen if he wished it to be so, and he realized that he didn't need to stay such a long distance away to remain unobserved. In time, he brought the ship closer and closer to his tribal brethren until he was able to actually hear their voices. What he heard at that point surprised him greatly.

He soon discovered that there was a great deal of love play among his tribe that he was completely unaware of. *How can this be?* he thought to himself as he witnessed his friends and family members shedding their deerskins and falling to the ground in a disgraceful display of writhing gyrations. Then his heart fell to the pit of his stomach as he witnessed Cesta Luna locked in a forceful fit of copulation with his own brother, Pinta Ceana, whose name meant *Horns of the Deer*.

Coal-Eyed Joe was furious. Before he could stop himself, the ship fired a series of light blasts into the screaming tribal orgy. Thirteen Miccosukee Indians were killed that day by what they thought were artillery rounds from the white devil's ships in the ocean. They had learned that the U.S. Navy had the capacity to fire artillery rounds from offshore, reaching well inland during the Second

Seminole War. The Seminole Wars, also known as the Florida Wars, were three conflicts in Florida between various groups of Native Americans, collectively known as Seminoles, and the United States. The First Seminole War was from 1817 to 1818, the Second Seminole War from 1835 to 1842, and the Third Seminole War from 1855 to 1858. The Second Seminole War, often referred to as "The Seminole War" lasted longer than any other war involving the United States between the American Revolution and the Vietnam War. It was from the historical accounts of these conflicts that Coal-Eyed Joe's people learned of the white devil's ability to strike from such a long distance. It had to be the white devils because they were the only ones who could rain down fire from the sky.

The indians had to do something. The Gods would look poorly upon a people who would allow such an evil act to go unpunished, so early one morning, ninety-seven white residents of Indian Key would pay the awful price with their lives.

After a considerable period of lamentation for both the members of his tribe and nearly one hundred innocent white people who were blamed for the attack, Coal-Eyed Joe decided that the only safe course of action was to remove the stone (and the ship) from the temptation of man. On a crisp December morning, he once again boarded his dugout cypress canoe and paddled a mile out to sea. He removed both of the control stones from the side cradles of the ship and used one of them to scuttle it to the bottom of the ocean. His mind *told* him that the ship lay in three thousand feet of water just off the island of Bimini. Without prayer or ceremony, he threw both of the stones with such force that he nearly capsized. A tear came to his eye as he watched them disappear beneath the sea.

All at once Kevin understood how the stone came to be amid the beach flotsam left on Melbourne Beach. Coal-Eyed Joe's attempt to rid mankind of the terrible temptation only lasted until the unwary interference of the Army Corps of Engineers. When sand was pumped in from a mile out at sea, along came the blue stone with all the other fossils which told their stories of the past. Kevin decided to make sure that the blue control stone's story would be told *only* to him and possibly Susan. He also decided that the time had come to make good on his promise of a demonstration. He heard about *"Peel's Observation,"* and knew that it was time to recall the ship.

A sudden realization also came to him regarding Susan's shocking experience at the concert over in Tampa. "You poor, baby," he said out loud to no one. Kevin knew that her sexual encounter was not her fault and not Doc Singer's either. It was the ship. First, it was the unwary Miccosukee Indians, and then the audience at the Dave Matthews concert. *The devil made them do it.* He finally understood how the ship affected animals and humans in its close proximity. It was an aphrodisiac. God didn't make a mere suggestion to go forth, be fruitful, and multiply. It was an irresistible imperative.

Whoever built the ship and let it loose upon the Earth fauna made sure that they had no choice in the matter. The ship stimulated the production of powerful pheromones. *If it weren't so tragic, it would be comical,* he thought. He chose at that instant to take Susan Lang into his colossal sphere of confidence.

~

July 14, 2005
11:54 P.M.
Indialantic, Florida

Kevin and Susan were standing by the shoreline on the beach at Two-Roads. It was the same stretch of lightless beach where Kevin tried unsuccessfully to bring the ship ashore on the night of July 8th. He placed his hands on her shoulders and looked deeply into her eyes.

"Sue, I have something to tell you."

"Sure," she said miserably. "Now, you want to marry me, right? Jesus, you have lousy timing, Murphy."

"I saw you at the Dave Matthews concert."

"What? You were spying on me?" she said hotly. "How dare you? You don't own me."

"Sue, would you just listen to me, I wasn't spying, exactly."

"Uh huh, just what *exactly* were you doing there?" her hands had found a resting place on her hips.

"I was a spectator, that's all. And it seems that I was a kind of instigator, too."

"What are you talking about, Kevin?"

"You weren't raped, Sue, and you weren't squirted with any roofie-laced, DMSO either."

"What could you possibly know about it?"

"I caused it, Sue. By accident. I caused the orgy."

"You're insane, you know that, don't you?"

"Just listen. I was there, but I wasn't on the ground. I didn't need a ticket, Sue. I was floating twenty feet *above* the stage. I had the best seat in the house."

"Oh, well that explains everything," she said rolling her eyes.

"I was in the ship, Sue – the alien ship – but it's not really aliens, it's just me."

"You're very lucky that I'm a doctor, Kevin, because you surely need one now."

"I have something wonderful to show you, Susan."

"What? What is it?" she asked wringing her hands. She was wondering if there was something seriously wrong with Kevin.

He reached into a small cloth bag he had been carrying and uncovered the stone making sure to hold it by the fabric. A moment later he asked her, "Well, what do you think?"

"Very nice," she said dryly. "So, what am I supposed to think?"

"Look at the color," he said.

"It looks dark blue. So?" she asked with a confused look on her face.

"Doesn't the color look familiar?" he prodded.

"Not particularly. What's this all about, Kevin?"

"It's the same color as the space ship. The one on TV."

"No, it's not. It's darker," She was starting to get angry.

"That's because it's night time!" he said excitedly.

"Kevin Murphy! What the hell are you talking about?"

"It's a control-stone. *Remote control.*"

"Oh, my God. You're not kidding, are you?" she said crossing her arms in front of her. Kevin knew it was an involuntary fear response. She began to shiver in the warm summer night air.

"I'm not kidding. Isn't it wonderful?" asked Kevin.

"Kevin, it's *evil*," she said.

"No it's not, Sue. It's just a tool."

"Sure. Just like the A-bomb."

"Oh, don't be so dramatic. Anyway, I've decided to get rid of it so no one can control it. I just wanted you to see it first."

"See it? You mean *see the ship*?" she asked.

"Sure, right now. Right here," he said.

"You're insane," she said matter-of-factly.

"That's another reason to get rid of it, but I'm okay, now. I got a little fuzzy for a while there, but now I'm fine."

"Jesus," she said. "You really plan to bring the space ship right here to Two-Roads, huh?"

"That's right."

"And then what?"

"We get in and go for a ride."

"You're nuts. What's gotten into you? Don't you think people will notice? You'll be arrested. You're now a criminal, Kevin."

"Look, Sue. I didn't mean to do anything wrong. It just got a little out-of-control, that's all. I can control it now, except I don't know how to stop all the pheromones."

"What pheromones?" she asked him.

"The ship has a rather curious effect on people when they get close enough. It makes them produce and react to pheromones."

"Why me?" Susan asked the sky with upraised arms.

"Here, Sue. Give me your hand," he said holding the stone out in front of him. He held it against his bare palm and placed her hand on top of it. Soon her eyes began to glass over and she said, "I think I feel something, Kevin," with a sudden impulse to take deeper breaths. "What *is* this that I'm feeling?" she asked.

"You're feeling me, Sue. And I'm feeling you. Isn't it wonderful?"

"Oh, yes," she said suddenly. "I think I know what you mean. I've never felt anything like it," she said breathing heavily.

"Oh, yes, you have," he told her. "The night of the concert, you felt the same thing, but you don't remember. I think the whole episode might erase itself from your conscious mind for some reason, but it's nice, isn't it?"

"Yes, it's very nice," she said. She reached up and kissed him on the lips.

"Hold on, Sue," he said slipping the stone back into the bag. As soon as the contact with the stone was broken, they both felt a sudden chill. All of a sudden, she seemed to be angry.

"My God, Kevin. Get rid of that awful thing," she said shivering.

"It's not so bad. What's so bad about wanting someone?"

"I'll tell you what's so bad about it. When I feel something for someone, I want it to be my idea, not some spaceman's. That thing is horrible, Kevin. It's evil, can't you see it?"

"I've done some good things, too, Susan. There's been a cessation of violence around the world. That's worth something, isn't it?"

"Of course. But you can't hope to control that thing. You won't be able to control yourself."

"I know. I just have one more thing to do. Then it's over."

"What is it that you plan to do," she asked with her hands on her hips.

"Destroy a battleship . . . from the moon."

"That's it. I'm outta' here," said Susan walking quickly away toward the dunes and their car.

"Susan! Wait!" he said running after her. He caught her and held her by putting his hands lightly on her shoulders, "Just hear me out, okay?"

"I'm listening," she said.

"It's all been arranged. The Navy has towed a cruiser out to sea, and the alien ship is going to demonstrate its ability to destroy it from the moon. Nobody's on it. Nobody's gonna' get hurt."

"But what's the point of it?" she asked.

"To put the fear of God back in them. I've told the world through the U.S. Air Force that I'll be keeping tabs on them. If they think I'm watching them from the dark side of the moon, they might just treat each other with a little more kindness. That's all I'm asking, Sue. I know world peace is out of the question, but couldn't we all treat each other with just a little more kindness?"

"You've spoken to them? How?"

"Remember the laptop you gave me. It talks."

"I know it talks," she said. A smile was trying to find her face when she asked, "Which voice did you use?"

"Zarvox."

"Oh, that's so corny. I wish I could have seen their faces."

"You can, Sue. Come with me."

"I don't know, Kevin. How can you be sure it's safe?"

"I've done it a bunch of times. Last time I went to the moon."

"The moon," she repeated deadpan.

"Sure. You've heard of Peel's observation?"

"Yes, but they didn't tell us what it was."

"It was the name of the ship. The one to be scuttled. I wrote it on the moon's surface. She's waiting patiently off the Virginia coast."

"So what will that prove?" she asked.

"The whole world will be watching."

Chapter Twenty-one
July 15, 2005
10:09 A.M.
Patrick Air Force Base, Satellite Beach, Florida

Kevin had persuaded Susan to board the ship with him. They flew to so many places around the Earth that Susan was in a dream-state with her eyes filling with tears, not really believing what she was seeing most of the time.

They went to the Great Pyramids of Giza, the top of Mount Everest, The Ross Sea in Antarctica, as well as the Red Square and the White House. The ship's ability to blend in with the night sky made them nearly invisible, so they escaped detection in every circumstance. Early the next morning, they found themselves hovering ten feet over runway one-eight-zero at Patrick Air Force Base.

Satellite Beach was beginning to suffer the wrath of Tropical Storm turned Hurricane Freda. General Hightower was accompanied by his driver, Sergeant Jim Sherman, as well as twenty airmen who once again surrounded the alien ship. The airmen made motions to protect their faces from the piercing raindrops, sparse though they were, but the general stood firmly in place, the consummate portrait of defiance. More inclement elements were no match for the man.

"I see that you have complied with my request of placing a battleship off your coastline," typed Kevin from the ship.

"The *U.S.S. Valiant.* You plan to scuttle her, is that correct?"

"*Yes.*"

"When can we expect this to take place?"

"How long will it take to align your satellite communications in order for all nations to witness the event?" asked Kevin. Susan was sitting calmly in the seat beside him. The ship was *teaching* her as well. She knew that although the view screen seemed translucent, the general couldn't see them inside the ship.

"I'll find out," said the general. He lifted a portable transmitter from the dashboard of the jeep. After speaking for about three minutes, he replaced it and turned to speak to the ship, "I'm told that it will take about twenty minutes to verify that all the affiliates are getting the satellite feed. Will that be satisfactory?"

"That will be fine. The Valiant will be dispatched in precisely thirty-five minutes."

Kevin and Susan took off from the Air Force Base and proceeded toward Earth's moon. The view was spectacular. Their canopy enabled them to see objects from impossible distances. The crab nebula in the constellation of Orion was a blazing red and orange miasma of swirling gasses as they appeared twenty thousand years ago. They were literally looking backward in time across a moveable event-horizon. The more intense their concentration, the further back in time they could see.

The image of the Earth quickly reduced in size as they completed their journey out and in. The two traversed the cosmos as easily as one would gaze across a star chart. When they reached the rings of Saturn, they paused to watch the many colored gasses and ice particles bouncing off their ship. They let the magnetic and gravitational fields pull them closer to the surface of the huge planet. When they lightly touched down, their ship displaced the landmass as though floating on the surface of a great sea. It wasn't solid ground, but a mixture of denser gasses and icy iron particles held together by the planet's huge gravitational forces. If the rotation of the planet on its axis could somehow be slowed down, it would be reduced to half its size with twice its density.

The ship had become a tutor and tour guide rolled into one. Their questions were satisfied, if not directly answered, the instant they were posed.

~

July 15, 2005
10:34 A.M.
Wuestoff Medical Center

Judy Murphy was propping her husband's pillow in Room 310. She had turned on the television set and tuned to WCIX for the coverage of the alien ship's demonstration. The cameras were trained on the *U.S.S. Valiant* from the Coast Guard Cutter *Sawfish* at anchor roughly a mile toward the leeward coast of Virginia. The *U.S.S. Farragut* was making twelve knots on the surface by slicing easily through a three-to-five-foot chop. She circled the old heavy cruiser holding a steady half-mile radius. The *Valiant* had often seen action as part of the sixth fleet in the Pacific theater during World War II. She served her country well and was now serving all of mankind with the ultimate sacrifice. A watery grave for a ship was a fitting end as it created more life in the form of an artificial reef to support a number of complex ecosystems. Kevin's sense of ecological consciousness is what gave him the idea in the first place. His demonstration would kill two birds with one stone.

Judy motioned to the television screen and said, "Aren't you glad you're in a nice warm bed instead of out there in that terrible weather, Kev?"

"Oh, it's not that bad out there. This storm's nothing. *Now, Andrew. That* was a storm," said her husband. "Where's Kevin, Judy? I hope he doesn't think he has to drive up here in this mess."

"I'm not sure, Hon. I'll bet he's holed up somewhere high and dry."

~

July 15, 2005
10:35 A.M.
Earth's Moon
The Sea of Tranquility

Kevin and Susan were sitting at the bottom of a large crater.

"Can you read the letters, Sue?"

"*U.S.S. V...al..iant. Valiant.* What does it mean?" she was looking out of the ship's canopy at the letters that Kevin had inscribed in the lunar moonscape two days before.

"It's the name of the ship. The one we're going to sink."

"Are you sure that no one will get hurt?" she asked.

"Sure, I'm sure," he said with an acquired confidence.

"Look at that storm. There in the Atlantic," said Susan pointing toward the Earth. "It looks pretty bad."

"Want to fix it?"

"What do you mean?"

"Here," he said. "Give me your hand." Kevin took Susan's hand and placed it on a small, very smooth stone located on the ship's center console. It was just in front of the control stone, which had turned gray to match the color of the moon's surface. The outer layer of the ship was now gray as well. The small stone was a weapons control station and began to teach Susan about its capabilities.

~

July 15, 2005
10:36 A.M.
Ten miles off the coast of Virginia

The wind was up and whitecaps were interwoven throughout the rolling swells of the sea. They were beginning to feel the first effects of Hurricane Freda whose sustained winds of eighty miles per hour classified her as a Category 1 storm. The eyes of the world were on the *Valiant* with the exception of the National Weather Service in Melbourne, Florida. *Their eyes were on Freda.*

If the force of Freda increased to a Category 2 storm before the completion of the demonstration, a storm surge could produce a series of wave swells capable of crippling the Coast Guard Cutter *Sawfish*. The Coast Guard would have no choice but to order her return to shore, leaving only the Ohio class submarine, *U.S.S. Farragut*, to document the event.

Fortunately, a small company based in Melbourne called North American Catastrophe Services recently developed the necessary equipment for the Navy. The Farragut was capable of photographing the *Valiant* with the use of a 30-foot telescoping boom equipped with a small gyroscope to keep the image still. However, wave peaks during a storm surge would obscure the image of the heavy cruiser for short periods of time. No one was sure how long it would take the alien craft to scuttle her. If it were merely seconds, the lesson could fall on blind eyes and deaf ears if the timing were off.

So far luck was with them, and the cutter *Sawfish* seemed to be holding her own with a storm anchor pointing her into the wind. The seamen on deck were miserable. The rolling of the ship on the great swells was a constant source of nausea for all of the men on board. The air wasn't cold but a biting wind forced rain at such a speed that their faces were stung whenever they were exposed.

Photographing the heavy cruiser from the wheelhouse of *Sawfish* was ruled out because the rain pounding the glass produced a blurry image from the cameras. The crews were forced to brave the elements tying themselves and their equipment to the slippery steel of the railing stanchions and deck cleats.

~

July 15, 2005
10:38 A.M.
Earth's Moon
The Sea of Tranquility

"Let it talk to you, Sue," said Kevin. "Think about it. How can you counteract the forces of the storm below us? What is it you want the ship to do?"

"Slow the motion," she said, "the circular motion of the wind. I want to *stop* the circular motion."

The ship came to life. A rapid pulsing sound began from somewhere deep inside the ship. Kevin and Susan could see light flashes emanating from the ship's exterior and shooting toward the storm in the Atlantic Ocean almost a quarter million miles below. The light was not continuous, but traveled on individual patches of the ether, which is the medium for electromagnetic radiation. It was as though a great hand was waving back and forth - interrupting the stream of light and producing individual balls instead of a constant beam.

The balls continued to fall in the path of the leading edge of the storm. At first it looked like they were falling harmlessly through the storm to the surface of the ocean. Then the swirling winds began to slow until the storm seemed to lose all definition. In a span of roughly four minutes, the storm was effectively reduced from a hurricane to a gentle rain.

~

July 15 2005

10:42 A.M.

Ten miles off the coast of Virginia

"This is WCIX reporter Bill Peters aboard the Coast Guard Cutter *Sawfish*. We have just witnessed a phenomenon of such magnitude that it dwarfs any natural weather event since the parting of the Red Sea. Hurricane Freda has effectively disappeared in a matter of minutes. The torrential rain and winds of more than eighty miles per hour have slowed to a light drizzle in a gentle breeze. We are now seeing the promise of a sunny day. *It is nothing short of incredible.* This reporter has never witnessed anything so stunning in an entire career in journalism. It is truly a miracle unparalleled in any notion of the modern era. *God bless us all.*"

July 15, 2005

10:45 AM

Earth's Moon

The Sea of Tranquility

"Nice work, Sue," said Kevin.

July 15, 2005

10:46 A.M.

Wuestoff Medical Center

"Oh look, Hon, it's stopped raining. That's odd. Maybe we're in the eye of the storm," said Judy.

"Turn up the sound, Honey," said Kevin, Sr.

Judy Murphy turned the up the volume on the hospital room's television set. The reporter, Bill Peters, was talking excitedly about the fierce storm suddenly subsiding.

"Storms don't just disappear," said her husband, "and God doesn't intervene. It's got to be the ship."

"What?"

"The space ship. It stopped the hurricane as part of the demonstration. If it can stop a weather phenomenon, it can certainly start one, also. It can hold us hostage with our own weather systems.   Hurricanes, earthquakes, typhoons, you name it!"

"By God, I think you're right, Kev," said Judy.

"By *somebody*, but it's certainly not God."

Chapter Twenty-two
July 15, 2005
10:49 A.M.
Earth's Moon
The Sea of Tranquility

"You want to take out the ship?" asked Kevin.

"Are you sure nobody's on it."

"Uh huh."

"How do you know, Kevin?"

"Ask the ship; let it *tell you* who's on board."

Susan placed her hand on the small smooth stone once again and cleared her mind. She let her thoughts drift to the ship and then wondered if it was truly empty. The answer filled her mind. It became her thought as though she had the answer all along.

The cruiser was empty or, at least, devoid of humans. There were a few bilge rats, roaches and silverfish, but nothing to be concerned about within a half-mile radius. She concentrated on restricting the pulses of light to within a quarter-mile of the cruiser and mentally released the reins of the ship. The response was immediate; however, the pulses weren't as intense as the first time she used them against the storm. Still, they were more than adequate to do the job. The old cruiser began to turn a reddish rust color and then the waterline started to lose its definition in a small cloud of steam. Soon the water churned in a rapid roiling boil and the great seams of the old steel plates began to lose their rivets and give way. She slid silently into the sea. The only sound was a fierce hissing noise by the superheated metal that was quickly cooled as it went under.

"Will you look at that!" said Bill Peters. "The heavy cruiser *U.S.S. Valiant* has been reduced to any number of rusty steel plates that have apparently no cohesion or organization whatsoever. It's as though the integrity of the ship was suddenly and completely compromised. It would seem that this awesome force could reduce even the most formidable ships to rubble in very short order. There is no doubt that any type of aircraft, tanks, or artillery forces would suffer the same fate. This is a wake-up call for us all. A warning that we have no choice but to heed. There apparently was no concussion force as the event was nearly silent. The battleship simply ceased to be. This is WCIX reporter, Bill Peters, signing off. *God help us all.*"

Shanice Williams was once again at the anchor desk back at WCIX studios. Her mood was somewhat pensive as she quietly said, "That was Bill Peters aboard the Coast Guard Cutter *Sawfish* bringing you the live picture of the destruction of a United States battleship. The ship was laid at anchor ten miles off the coast of Virginia out of Norfolk Naval Base. Also witnessing the demonstration at the scene was the Ohio Class Nuclear Submarine, *U.S.S. Farragut*. There apparently was no collateral damage to either vessel as the alien craft deeply drove home the point of its superiority. We can only hope that the demands of our distant neighbors will not be too costly. This is Shanice Williams for WCIX news. Rest assured that we will keep you abreast of any further developments."

~

July 15, 2005
11:00 A.M.
Earth's Moon
The Sea of Tranquility

"*That* was an exhilarating sensation, Kevin."

"It was necessary, Susan. We had to demonstrate that we mean business."

"You mean *we* the aliens?"

"Of course."

"But it's all a lie," said Susan.

"Do you want to tell them the truth?"

"I'm not sure what I want to do, Kevin. One thing I am sure of is that we need to keep this ship *only under our command*. This is too big for any singular interest. Do you understand me?"

"Of course, I do, but I'm afraid that it's too big a power for the two of us as well."

"What are you talking about," said Susan.

"Just listen to yourself, Sue. You said you were jazzed by the power!"

"Well, of course, I was jazzed. But that doesn't mean I can't handle the reality of the situation. We are the benefactors. We are the minds that can direct the true path of a progressive and peaceful society."

"You know what you sound like?" asked Kevin.

"I know, Stalin, but you know better than that."

"Do I?"

"We are benevolent. We're non-violent. But we must have the power to back up our demands," said Susan.

"I think we've backed up enough demands for now," said Kevin. "We've obliterated a United States battleship."

"Yes, but only for a demonstration. We let them sacrifice an asset that was ineffective and inconsequential to the collective forces of the United States."

"So now we can quit, right, Susan?"

"Yes, for now," she said.

"What do you mean for now?"

"Oh, don't be such a simpleton, Kevin. The craft is bigger than both of us. You *know* that. We have to keep it on hand for any number of reasons..."

"There. You see it? It's captured you, Susan. You don't even sound like you."

"What do you mean," said Susan. "It's your monster. I'm just along for the ride."

"Wait a minute. I love you with all my heart. Could we just focus on that for the time being?"

"I don't know, Kevin. Your baggage is just a little bit heavy right now."

"Well, why don't we just forget it, Sue. How 'bout I drop you off at Two Roads tonight and we call it quits?"

"I think we have to have a pact."

"What do you mean?" asked Kevin.

"No one uses the ship without the other person," she said.

"A pact won't be necessary, Sue."

"Why, what do you mean?"

"The only way you can use the ship is with me."

"What are you talking about, Kevin. I can just take the stone and use the ship or misuse the ship any way I want."

"Won't work."

"Huh?"

"You can't remove the stone. Neither can anybody else, except me."

"Are you sure?" she asked.

"Pretty sure. I felt it the first time I opened the ship. It scanned my DNA, and now mine is the only hand that can take the stone away or put it back in the cradle. It just won't work for anybody else."

"So, I can't use the stone, is that right?"

"Not unless you have my DNA."

"What if I cut off your hand?" she asked.

"Let's not go there, okay, Susan. You're starting to creep me out."

"So, you're the only one who can use the ship?" she asked.

"Oh, no, you can use it all right. Anybody can. All you have to do is *touch* the stone and the canopy will open right up for you."

"So why wouldn't I?"

"Because you can't *hide* it. *I'm* the only one who can remove the stone, at least for now until another pilot succeeds me. I'm not looking forward to that because I'm pretty sure that would mean that I'm dead."

"What's the purpose of that?"

"I think it's a safeguard. If you can't remove the stone, you can't hide the ship unless you're in it."

"I just don't get it," said Susan. "What are we supposed to be *doing* with the ship? What's its purpose?"

"I think it's supposed to spread life; to encourage or compel life to become greater in number - all of life."

"That's it?"

"That's a lot," said Kevin. "Suppose you wanted to seed a planet with life, but were unsure whether there would be sufficient motivation for procreation. You've heard people say things like, *'I don't want children'* or *'I wouldn't bring a child into this world,'* haven't you?"

"Yeah, so?"

"Well, I think the ship might change their mind. If they get close enough, they have a compulsion to react to pheromones. Hell, I think the thing actually makes us create pheromones. How do you feel when you touch the stone with your bare hand, Susan?"

"I want to have your children, Kevin, *lots of them* - whether we're married or not."

"See?"

"It's all too confusing, Kevin. A ship as powerful as that has to have a more important purpose than that."

"What's more important than the continuation of life?"

"I'm not so sure what's important anymore. If we had children, would it be for the right reason? Would it even be our idea?" she asked miserably.

"I don't know about anything anymore," he said. "All I'm sure of is that I love you, with or without the damned stone."

"Are you sure?" she asked.

"When we get rid of the damned thing, we'll find out, won't we?"

"Are you sure we can?"

"Yeah, I'm sure. It's been nothing but trouble since I found it. But first things first."

"What do you mean?"

"We have to go back to Patrick now."

"What for?" she asked.

"To tell the general that we stopped Freda in her tracks. That was a stronger argument than scuttling the ship."

"What do you mean?"

"It's simple. If we can stop a destructive weather pattern, we could also start one, couldn't we?"

"Yes, but we would never do that, Kevin."

"But *they* don't know that."

July 15, 2005

11:05 AM

Patrick Air Force Base

Kevin and Susan were talking to General Hightower on runway one-eight-zero, *"Were your observations successful, General?"*

"I believe so. The scuttling of the ship was recorded by a number of cameras. It was also witnessed live via satellite throughout the world. I believe you have made a very strong point."

"And the weather system that threatened your coastline?"

"That was your doing, I take it."

"Would you like it to return? It can be arranged."

"That won't be necessary. You've made an effective demonstration. I believe that many nations will cease hostilities for fear of reprisals from your people. You've won."

"We shall see. We will be watching from the dark side of your moon."

"I will pass along the information," said the general.

Chapter Twenty-three
July 15, 2005
11:10 A.M.
Ecuador

Kevin and Susan left the air force base and flew directly to the Galapagos Islands. They wanted to see a rare bird called the Blue-footed Booby. It afforded them a slight break in the hot weather because the direct rays of the sun were closer to the Tropic of Cancer than the equator. They exited the ship and then quickly moved it out to sea with the control stone. They walked the trails of the biggest island. Tortoise nests were visible along the eastern dunes. The rising moon would guide the hatchlings to the sea as long as the boobies were asleep. It was a cruel world out there for the hatchlings. If the birds didn't get them, there was always the chance that the seals, rays or sharks would. All part of the nitrogen chain. Ashes to ashes - chum to chum. Kevin and Susan walked along the beach holding hands. Susan stopped suddenly and pulled Kevin close to her. He could feel the rise and fall of her breath against his skin. She looked deeply into his eyes, "There has to be a reason for all of this."

"The reason is because I chose you to share it with."

"Yeah, but what are the odds that *you* would find the stone?"

"A trillion to one, I guess."

"A trillion to one," she repeated.

"It means that we were destined to share a bond more powerful than anything in the history of this planet."

"It seems that way doesn't it," she said.

"You know I love you, Susan."

"You've told me a number of times."

"And how do you feel?" he asked.

"You know I love you, too, Kevin. It's just that I don't know how I feel about all of this right now. I mean, look at the situation. We are fugitives from justice or at least you are. You've destroyed government property - enough to send you to jail for about a hundred years or so. We've destroyed a U.S. battleship together. Now *I'm* a criminal. We're effectively holding the nations of the world for ransom, even though the only thing we want is for them to stop killing each other. It's all too much to digest all at once.

The only thing I'm sure of is that we can't *ever* let them know who we are. That would be suicide. We have to be ultra careful, Kevin. We have to use the ship very sparingly and be very careful not to hurt anybody."

"What if we have to back up our demands?" he asked.

"We'll cross that bridge when we come to it. Who knows, maybe nature will do a lot of it for us. We've reduced the world to the dark ages," she said. "We're the Gods of the bad juju. If there's an earthquake, maybe they'll think that the Gods are angry."

"Well, maybe the world *will* make you angry, Sue. You ever think of that? I'm sure you've been incensed from time to time about the insanity and cruelty around the world. You could never do anything about it before, so you've never asked yourself the question of what you would do if you could. Now you have to ask the question."

"You're probably right, Kevin. But not *right* now."

"What else do you have to do right now, Susan?"

"Love you," she said.

"I like the sound of that," he said.

The Earthly Gods embraced their passion in the sand and the surf. They suddenly had a terrible purpose. Something they had avoided for most of their lives. It was such a luxury to just blend in with society, become invisible and let the world take care of itself. Now they were self-appointed caretakers of the world. They could punish acts of evil with nothing more than a notion of propriety. Kevin had learned the hard way that his responsibility could be compromised as easily as a thought could be formed.

The pressure was huge and with it came a dangerous side effect. It was the development of a God complex. They both had it. Any sober thinking individual would be making moves to remove the craft from the control of *any* human. Kevin had the instinct to do just that, but he later justified the continued access to control of the ship. He knew deep in his heart that he would never give up the power now. Neither would Susan. After all, they were only human . . . weren't they? Only time would tell.

Kevin had already begun to sow the seeds of compromise. He believed that the two of them could mine diamonds by merely flying through gem-rich mountains and gathering the fruits of their travels. It made little difference to him that the mining rights didn't belong to him. Why not fly through Fort Knox, for that matter? Somehow it made a difference to him, possibly, because the African nations were always being exploited by American interests. Their rationalization was that they were just picking up where the Europeans left off.

But then what was Kevin going to do with raw, uncut diamonds. He abandoned that particular scheme, but it set a dangerous precedent. It would eventually lead to a casual disregard for subtlety, which was sure to be fraught with danger and destructive implications. He would eventually take more and greater chances until they both were caught. It was the natural progression of absolute power - to push the envelope with unnecessary chances. He knew that Susan was not immune to it either. He found himself wondering if Susan knew where Brenda's house was situated in Vero Beach. He was afraid she might decide to do some remodeling.

"Sue."

"What?" she asked.

"I need to ask you something."

"Fire away," she said.

"You're not gonna' like it."

"Oh, would you just ask the question for God's sake."

"When Brenda called you. What did she say?"

Susan started to laugh hysterically. She found that she couldn't stop herself. When she started to speak the laughter just exploded out of her again and again.

"Oh, come on, Sue. What did she say?" Kevin was becoming a little miffed.

When Susan was finally able to control herself she said, "She said that you'd never make any kind of impact on the world."

"Really? She said that?"

"Uh huh."

They both laughed hysterically rolling in the surf with the Blue-footed Boobies and seals looking on.

Chapter Twenty-four
July 15, 2005
1:54 P.M.
Patrick Air Force Base

Colonel Cliff Byrd and a very nervous General Steven Hightower were in the general's office conducting a conference call with the Oval Office at the White House. President Conner Powell asked, "Your assessment, Steven?"

"Sit tight, for now. They've got the high cards, Mr. President."

"The high cards? What the hell is that supposed to mean?" asked Powell.

"Superior firepower, that's what. Superior flight ability, superior weaponry, you name it. Do you want to force me to send some of our best men on a suicide mission? What would we gain?"

"I don't like someone dictating to us what we can and can't do, General."

"Well, do you think I like it either? We're looking at our options, Mr. President. However, any action we take is likely to endanger our own citizens, either through collateral damage or possible repercussions," said the general.

"We have to hit them hard, General. A knock-out punch so to speak."

"We're working on it, Mr. President."

"Well, keep me posted, Steven."

"Will do."

The General terminated the connection with the White House. He asked his good friend and second in command, "Do you think he's serious, Cliff?"

"Sounded like it to me, Steven."

"It's crazy. Isn't it?"

"I guess. I don't know. Maybe we can take the thing out," said the colonel.

"He's talking about nukes, you know that, Cliff."

"I know."

"They won't let us kill, so we nuke them. What kind of sense does that make, Clifford?"

"It's our job to kill, Steven. They won't let us do our job. That's the real rub. For years we were the almighty morality police of the world. We were the architects of the new world order. I think we've just got a huge prescription of our own medicine."

"Unfortunately, our commander and chief isn't going to swallow it," said the general.

"Which means he might get us all killed."

"That's right. That's why they call it war, Cliff."

"War with the aliens? That's madness. Someone has to stand up to Powell. He needs to understand what we're up against. Has he seen the films?" asked the colonel.

"I don't know, but I would think so. What he really needs to see is what happened to the causeways. They flew *through* them.   What's to stop them from flying through the Capital building or the White House?   He's just not thinking straight, Cliff, but let's give him a little time."

"Are you going to arm a nuclear warhead on a fighter, Steven?"

"Of course, not."

~

July 15, 2005
2:15 P.M.
Melbourne Beach, Florida

The house that Kevin and Susan lived in on Third Avenue had one dominant feature - a mango tree. Covering almost half of the back yard was a large mango tree with nearly a fifty-foot canopy. Kevin assured Susan that he could descend to their back yard from six thousand feet in a matter of seconds. They were hovering directly over their house, looking down beside their seats through a transparent floor. It gave them the eerie feeling that they were floating on air without the ship to support them. The floor also had the telescopic properties of the canopy above them.

When they scrutinized their house's immediate area, they found it to be relatively quiet with no sign of any human activity. After some mild dissension from Susan, Kevin was finally able to overcome her resistance. They decided to try it. Their descent took less than fourteen seconds. When they stopped just short of the ground, they were only mildly pressed into the padding of their seats. The stealth properties of the craft prevented anyone from witnessing the event. Along with the color change or cryptic mimicry of the craft, Kevin was relieved to learn that the skin was photo-reflective as well. The same small photographic cells that enabled the magnification of objects on the view screen projected a real-size image on the opposite side of the craft. It effectively became invisible for all intents and purposes. As an added precaution, Kevin slowly moved the craft beneath the mango tree and gently settled it into the sandy soul. When the top of the ship's canopy was precisely even with ground level, he slid forward on his seat. The ship silently opened and the two space travelers got out. Kevin removed the control-stone from the port side of the ship and the canopy closed again. Susan took the stone from him and entered the house through the back yard sliders. Kevin used the many leaves dropped by the mango tree to hide any evidence of the ship. They'd done it. It was a big risk; however, their lack of caution was something not entirely in their control. It was as though they couldn't help themselves. Their arrogance was increasing as they evolved into something they wouldn't have considered a short time ago. They began to think of themselves as superior to normal human beings. They even dared to suggest a name for what they were becoming. *The Guardians of Harmony*, and then finally,

The Guardians of the Way. They had become drunk with power and were losing a half-hearted battle to fight the addiction.

As with any addiction, there was the rationalization of its necessity, thereby, an excuse for its continuation. Their personalities were effectively lost. Susan began canceling her appointments, and Kevin called the builders he was working for and told them he had found other work. They had enough money saved between them to last until they could devise a way to use the ship for their own gain. It was necessary, they reasoned, to support *The Guardians of the Way.*

The international news section of their local paper became their unwitting accomplice. They responded to the first headline:

"Saddam Hussein Tests Long-range Missile.*"* It seemed that Saddam Hussein didn't heed their warning. The only use Iraq would have for a long-range weapon was to deliver a warhead for mass destruction, either biological or nuclear. They felt it was their job to punish them for their actions. Although Iraq was already suffering from the aftermath of the Gulf War, The Guardians decided to hit them in the pocketbook. They first engaged in slow-flight over the no-fly zone of Iraq. This brought about anti-aircraft fire as they chose not to employ the ship's stealth apparatus. They returned fire to the radar and anti-aircraft installations by dissolving the magnetic field properties of their equipment. No one was injured; however, their war machine was sorely compromised as all their anti-aircraft missiles were completely destroyed. They could have stopped there, but they thought they had to drive home a point that they were not to be disobeyed. Saddam's palaces were next. Four of them were completely obliterated by the alien craft. They would read in the paper the next day that seven civilians were killed in the attacks.

"Do you believe it?' Susan asked Kevin.

"I didn't sense any loss of life. It's probably just propaganda."

"Probably? Is that good enough? Are we killing people now?"

"Not on purpose, Sue. But suppose we just saved thousands of lives by discouraging their development of the missiles. Doesn't that count for anything?"

"I'm not sure," she said. "We better go slow, Kevin."

"We are going slow. And as far as being sure, you will be. The next time an Iraqi sponsored terrorist action is targeting innocent American citizens."

"I guess you're right."

"Of course, I'm right. *I'm a Guardian.*"

Susan wasn't sure she liked the sound of that. She envisioned a future when the term *Guardian* might be synonymous with *Tyrant*. The next time they reacted to the newspaper headlines the infraction was much more grave and specific.

"North Korea Threatens To Abandon Armistice." The world's most heavily armed border between North and South Korea was poised for a conflict not seen for fifty years. The Armistice Agreement began in lieu of a peace treaty following the 1950-1953 Korean War. North Korea had recently proven their capabilities for deployment of a nuclear weapon to the United States and stated that the imminent blockade of Korean Naval activity to undermine the development of a nuclear program would constitute an act of war. Confident that the Korean's anti-aircraft weaponry would be as ineffective as the Iraqi's had been, The Guardians were intent on flying over the hotbed border and dismantling the weapons of both sides.

On this occasion, they did so from twenty-thousand feet high. They also employed their stealth capabilities to prevent a possible nuclear assault. The operation took a little over three hours. Seventeen hundred tanks and artillery vehicles were reduced to impotent piles of metal and electronic circuitry. The armies on both sides of the border were largely unharmed; however, some casualties were reported the next day.

"We did it again, Kevin," said Susan. "It says ninety men and women killed in the attacks."

"What do you want to do, Susan, quit? It's probably just another lie. Do you really think we should quit now? We're so close."

"Are we? Do you think nations will learn lessons from each other's punishment? We'll end up punishing every country in the world before we're through," she said.

"If we have to, we have to. That way the people who have suffered *'accidents'* won't have died in vain," he argued.

"But do we have the right?"

"To end suffering? Of course, we do."

"To end free will. That's what we would be doing. Putting an end to the fear of God. Why fear God when you first have to fear *The Guardians?"* she said miserably. "It's all going wrong, Kevin."

"Just stick with it, Sue. Or, at least, just don't stop me."

"I can't let you do it by yourself – I can't let you take all of the blame. I'm a part of it now, and I'll see it through with you. But please. We have to find a way to be gentler. We need to focus on non-living targets. No more casualties. Let's be creative."

"I'm glad you mentioned that. I have an idea."

"Oh, boy," she said warily. "Here we go."

"I think you're gonna like this one, Sue. You get to be an international art thief."

"Just what I've always wanted," she said dryly.

Chapter Twenty-five
July 19, 2005
2:13 A.M.
The London Art Museum

"**A**re you sure it's here," asked Susan.

"Yes. I even know what room it's in. I was here about four months ago on a golf trip. A buddy of mine lives here."

The Guardians were on the roof of The London Art Museum. A silent pulse of light obliterated the lock on the steel door leading to the fire stairwell. Kevin left the craft and Sue stayed behind in case he encountered any unexpected trouble. They knew that the museum was empty during the night except for a single guard in a front office by the Museum's gift shop. The painting that Kevin was after was in one of the rear rooms. The room had no windows to protect the paintings from ultraviolet light. There were also no alarms. Taking the painting was child's play. The only hard part was stilling his rampaging heart. It was displayed in an alcove all by itself. When he took it from the wall, he noticed that the frame was only attached by four small wing nuts. The painting came away easily, and he replaced the frame back on the wall. It was so simple. It was truly a national treasure, yet so easy to obtain. He was actually holding Vincent Van Gogh's *Starry Night* in his hands. When he reached the roof, Susan opened the canopy for him. She looked at the painting as he positioned it behind their seats. There, stapled to a simple wooden frame, was a painting worth over ninety million dollars.

"It's beautiful," she said.

"It sure is. Let's get out of here."

Susan piloted the ship straight up into the night and back to their home in Melbourne Beach, Florida. The greatest art theft in the history of mankind took less than an hour. It was time to compose a letter to the company that insured the painting. The ransom would be nominal. Simply a world at peace. A detailed list of all the assets that the company insured would accompany the letter. When they discovered that the lock on the fire-stairway door had been decomposed in the same manner as the weapons in Iraq and Korea, there would be little doubt as to who had the painting. The implication was obvious. Nothing was safe. Nothing was beyond their reach. The craft could hold any treasure for ransom. Unfortunately, The Guardians had finally tipped their hand.

~

July 20, 2005
8:45 AM
Patrick Air Force Base

Why that painting? Why any painting. They had to have known of its value. What kind of alien would covet art from an Earthling? General Hightower was once again on the phone with the Oval Office, "They made their first mistake, Mr. President."

"What do you mean, General?"

"The painting. To covet the painting is all too human. Why not take a number of paintings from the gallery? I'm convinced that we're dealing with at least one human, if not all humans, involved with the alien ship."

"You may be right, but how does that help our situation?"

"I'm not sure it does, but we may be better able to negotiate an end to their interference."

"I'm not sure I follow your logic," said Powell.

"If they're human, they have to answer to an angry God just as we do. *Forgive us our trespasses as we forgive those who trespass against us.* The concept is pretty deeply rooted, Mr. President."

"I go to church, General."

"We are not allowed to pass judgment here on Earth. That is for *The Lord* to do," said the general.

"And if they're Jewish?"

"Same thing."

"Muslim?"

"The same. Terrorists are not true Muslims, Mr. President."

"Hindu? Buddhist? Roman Catholic?" asked the President.

"Nada," said Hightower. "The Spanish Inquisition's over, Mr. President. No one on Earth has the right to judge our actions, at least not objectively. They have to look at the situation from the inside. Therefore, they are not qualified to judge."

"Provided they're human," stated Powell.

"Provided they're human," agreed the general.

"Good work, Steven. Keep me posted."

"Thank you, Sir," said the general hanging up. He turned to the colonel by his side and said, "Our first break, Cliff."

"I hope so. You'd better hope that the aliens aren't art lovers, Steven. Maybe they just like Van Gogh. They say everybody likes Van Gogh."

"I don't like Van Gogh, Clifford. I'm more a Jackson Pollack man myself."

"I like Van Gogh," said the colonel.

Kevin Murphy and Susan Lang were enjoying a Van Gogh at that very moment. It was hanging on the wall above their sofa. If news of the theft became common knowledge, they supposed they would have to move it to the bedroom. They were becoming accustomed to taking risks. It made their lives more intense. Soon the intensity would lead the world to their doorstep if they weren't very careful. They could always escape in the ship; however, to be accountable for the ship's actions was unthinkable. They would be wanted for murder, vandalism, international grand larceny, as well as conspiracy to create international incidents. Not a bad rap sheet for just a few days. And it was getting longer. They needed to protect their terrible secret now more than ever if they hoped to survive. What began as good intentions were rapidly snowballing into something beyond their control. They had the might to confront the world but not without a high price to pay. Soon they would be unable to protect their anonymity. Then the only thing they would have left would be their love for each other. Something was telling them that it wouldn't be enough.

"Oh, my God!" shouted Susan. "It's all wrong."

"What?" asked Kevin. "What's wrong."

"How could we be so careless?" she asked miserably. "Shit, it's probably already too late."

"What are you talking about, Sue?"

"The ship. We have to move the ship back to West Melbourne."

"But it's invisible," argued Kevin.

"There's a heat signature. A big web by now and we're right in the middle of it."

"Sue, calm down. What is it that you're afraid of?"

"Picture this," she said. "Suppose you had satellite photos of Brevard County over the last few days and looked at only heat, not objects. It would show up as red lines from the infra-red end of the spectrum. They would appear as vectors. Heat signatures of all the movements of the ship."

"Oh, my God, you're right."

"You're damned right I am. Can you guess what it would look like if you overlay all of the photos?"

"A big red spider web with Third Avenue right in the center."

"We got too cocky, Kevin. *You* got too cocky."

"Calm down, Sue. We can move it back tonight."

"I hope to God it isn't too late."

"You may be getting all worked up over nothing, Sue. I don't remember us going supersonic anytime in the last week, do you?"

"No, not really, except when we went to the moon."

That heat signature would be a dot, not a line. I think we're in the clear."

"Still, I'd sleep better knowing the ship is bedded down in a nice cow pasture instead of in our back yard."

"You're right. For now, we'll just be careful not to go too fast around Third Avenue."

Chapter Twenty-six
July 20, 2005
8:36 A.M.
Patrick Air Force Base

G eneral Hightower was talking to the editor of the international news desk for the local paper, "I've just read it, Mr. Harding. It's very good, very well written. If I didn't know better, I'd believe every word of it," said the general.

"Wrote it myself, General. Once I got the call from The White House. Can you tell me what it's all about?"

"I'm afraid not. But rest assured, you've done your country a great service."

"If you say so, General. All I did was print a bunch of lies."

"Let's keep that between us for now, okay, Mr. Harding?"

"Sure thing, General."

Colonel Byrd was sitting in the general's office, "Think it'll work, Steven?"

"It has a good chance. If it does, we'll know I'm right." They were looking at a headline in the morning paper. It read, "**Libyans Strike Again.**" The story went on to tell of an explosion in a movie theater attended mostly by the families of American servicemen near a small Air Force installation in Turkey. The explosion was being attributed to Al Qatar, a radical Muslim organization in Libya, who apparently was taking credit for the attack. The story was a fabrication engineered by General Hightower to instigate an action by the alien craft.

~

July 20, 2005
9:05 A.M.
Melbourne Beach, Florida

Kevin was reading the headline to Susan, **"Libyans Strike Again."** His brow was wrinkled and she felt like she could see the wheels turning in his mind. "Looks like we have a little work to do over Tripoli," he told her.

"Oh, Kevin. I'm liking this less and less by the minute. How about another art treasure?" she asked hoping to change his mind.

"They were Americans, Sue. Some were only children. They have to learn that we mean business."

"Oh, all right," she said half-heartedly. "But I still don't like it."

The Guardians then set out in the craft for Libya. When they were almost there Susan asked him, "What is it you plan to do?"

"Same thing Regan did in the eighties. Destroy their infrastructure. Bridges, roads, factories, that kind of thing."

"What about the loss of life?"

"What comes around, goes around," said Kevin.

"Let's take a look at the theater that was destroyed."

"What for?"

"Just humor me. What was the name of the town?" she asked."

"Karaman," he said. "Southern Turkey, just north of the Taurus Mountains. The U.S. Air force has a temporary base on the plain just below the foothills. Shouldn't be too hard to find."

"Then let's find it. I want to see it before we destroy a city like Tripoli."

"What for?" asked Kevin.

"Just a hunch."

They were able to locate the airbase on the east-end of Karaman. Then they located the base housing community, and finally, the movie-theater itself. It was entirely intact. There had never been any explosion. Instantly, Kevin understood the ruse and was livid.

"Aren't you glad I asked you to see the movie theater?" she asked.

"I can't believe they would do that to us. We almost killed innocent people for no reason at all. All because they wanted to see if they could force our hand. Do *their* dirty work."

"But we were too smart for them."

"You were too smart, Sue. I was intent on action. Now that we know their game, we have to try to turn the table on them."

"What do you mean?" she asked

"It's back to the Air Force Base, Sue."

"But we can't exactly admit to reading the paper. That's how they were trying to trick us in the first place."

"You're right. Let's just go home and lay low for a while."

"Sounds good to me."

When they returned to Melbourne Beach, The Guardians put the ship to rest in the back yard and ordered a pizza. They relaxed in a loveseat opposite the couch sipping on a Columbia Crest Merlot and gazing up at Van Gogh's *Starry Night.*

"I think we should get a Monet for the dining room," said Kevin. "I was thinking of *Red Poppies.*"

"Where is it?" asked Susan.

"I'm not sure. It was in The National Gallery of Art in Washington, D.C., but I think it was just on loan. I know where there's a really nice Gauguin. *Agony in the Garden* is in a museum in Palm Beach. It's called the Norton Art Museum. Take us about ten minutes each way."

"I don't think so, Kevin. That's not even funny."

"I'm serious. We could do it."

"Not without drawing attention to ourselves. You have to give it a little more thought than that."

"You're right. That's what I love about you, Sue. You're the sensible one."

"Well, someone has to be. I'm not ready to give up my life as a human being just yet. I still like movies, restaurants, shopping malls, you know - normal stuff."

"Me too, Sue. I'll be careful, I promise," said Kevin. "Speaking of restaurants, where is that pizza?"

"It'll be here in a minute."

"Next time I'll take the ship and pick it up at the drive-thru."

"Kevin!"

"I'm just kidding. Geeze, Susan. Sometimes you've got no sense of humor."

The doorbell rang and Susan got up to meet the delivery boy. She made no move to hide the Van Gogh. Why bother, really? Anyone would assume it was only a print. The next prize they had in mind was the *Crown Jewels of England* from The Tower of London.

After a hit such as that, they would spare England from any of their activity for a while. They were toying with the idea of getting King Tut's burial mask. Then there was always *The Hope Diamond* from the Smithsonian, and of course, *The Mona Lisa* from the Louvre. In time, their little house would become rather crowded. Maybe they should consider building an addition. Possibly even another garage bay with a door that opened to the back yard.

It was fun to think about, but they knew it would never really happen. It was foolish to keep the Van Gogh in their house, but they really were enjoying it. They told themselves not to get too attached. It had to go into storage eventually along with all the other treasures they planned to take. Mankind would never be able to part with their precious *things*. If you threaten their lives, they might call your bluff. Human life has no inherent monetary value. On the other hand, threaten them with the destruction of their things, and you get their undivided attention. The biggest ace-in-the-hole was the deception that the ship was occupied by alien beings. It was fortunate that Susan was clever enough to suspect and discover that the general was trying to manipulate them.

There would be no more newspapers. There was no one they could trust except each other. Kevin told the general that they would be watching from the dark side of the moon. Any reprisals in the future had to be the result of first hand observation. The aliens certainly weren't getting a copy of the local paper. It was imperative that they would be able to perpetuate the ruse. Humans could never bring themselves to destroy the greatest treasures of mankind, but aliens could. They would mean nothing to them except a source of tools for coercion. Holding the world's great art for ransom. *It had a nice ring to it.*

Chapter Twenty-seven
July 29, 2005
10:04 A.M.
Patrick Air Force Base

The Guardians were, once again, speaking to General Hightower on runway one-eight-zero. Kevin was saying, *"We assume that you are aware of the fact that we now hold a great deal of your planet's art treasures."*

"Yes, that has been our conclusion. What is the purpose of your actions?" asked the general.

"Your species continues to prey on each other. If this continues, we are prepared to destroy all of the artifacts and begin collecting more. In time we will gather all the material objects that are desirable to your society and do away with them forever. Is that a scenario that appeals to you?"

"Of course not," said the general. "But it won't work. The people who have nothing won't care about the confiscated art. It means nothing to them."

"Then it is in your interest to make them care. A unified effort toward peace is the only thing that will save your treasured possessions. Perhaps it is time to redistribute the wealth of your society so the strong no longer take advantage of the weak. Then you will be able to retain your riches, but only after all of your people are

adequately cared for. It is your decision. As always, we will be watching. Your actions shall demonstrate your intentions. Further communication will, therefore, not be necessary."

Kevin and Susan lifted gently off the runway and slowly cruised over toward a large hanger that housed a B-2 Stealth Bomber. The state of the art aircraft was one of the jewels of the armed forces and the movement clearly got the attention of the general. All of a sudden, light pulses began emanating from many different points on the outer surface of the alien craft. The huge hanger began to vibrate and turn an angry shade of red. Then, one whole side of the building collapsed down into a perfectly straight line of fine powder. The mighty Stealth Bomber was entirely exposed for all to see. Nothing was sacred, and nothing was safe. Small wisps of smoke rose in the air from the ashes of the fallen framework and panels of the building. The alien craft then rose quickly out of site. Kevin and Susan had the distinct impression that their little demonstration was not lost on the general.

"Did you see the look on his face?"

"I think you're enjoying this a little too much," said Susan.

"You know what they say, *love your work*."

"Speaking of work, any ideas?"

"It's time we went back overseas," he said.

"The Middle East?"

"I'd say so. What do *you* think?"

"I'd say we're overdue," she said.

The Guardians' first stop was Iraq. The Iraqi army was in tatters. Their uniforms were dirty and threadbare, and their general health was poor. To think that they were on the brink of war with the world's strongest superpower was ludicrous. They were being held-hostage by their own leader, Saddam Hussein. His agenda was to bring the other Arab-nations into a jihad or holy war with the Americans. The point was to punish America for supporting Israel with respect to their Palestinian conflict. The Jewish influence in America was never going to wane, and the pressure on the powers-that-be was enormous. The hands of the American people were tied at every turn. They couldn't support their leaders in a war effort against an inferior enemy. A preemptive strike by Americans was unprecedented. Still, they couldn't support the actions of maniacal leaders of rogue nations like Saddam Hussein. Their defiance of The United Nation's demands to disarm themselves could not be ignored.

The American people could not turn a blind eye to the threat of terrorism within their own borders in the wake of the September 11th attacks on the World Trade Center and The Pentagon. There was no clear position with which to be comfortable. Unless you were The Guardians with their unwavering position: peace, at any cost. That was their only agenda. It wasn't oil or Jews or Palestinians or American interests. It was simply peace by whatever means possible.

When they entered the no-fly zone over Iraq, there was no anti-aircraft fire even though they remained visible to both radar and the naked eye. It seemed that their previous encounter either eliminated their entire anti-aircraft missile capabilities or else demonstrated the futility of firing at the strange craft. In either case, they met no resistance.

Within minutes, a U.S. Air Force F-16 screamed by them at nearly Mach-1. They didn't see it coming because they were focusing all of their attention on the military installations below. They increased their speed to match the fighter and stayed about a half-mile behind. They were traveling roughly six hundred ninety miles per hour at an altitude of three thousand feet. Suddenly they saw the fighter fire two laser-guided missiles at mobile artillery units on the ground. The speed of thought proved to be much faster than the speed of a missile produced by expanding gasses. Light pulses from the alien craft overtook the missiles in an instant and reduced them to their elementary components without so much as a pop. They fell to Earth as dust clouds to the excited cheers of the Iraqi soldiers below. The fighter then fired again, and again the light pulses reduced the missiles to powder.

The official position of the American government is that in order to enforce the no-fly zone, it is necessary to fire on radar installations with anti-aircraft capabilities *when they are fired upon.* It is clearly defined as a position of self-defense only. Since the Iraqi soldiers were not firing at either the fighter or the alien craft, the Americans had no right to fire their missiles at ground installations. According to the rules of engagement, they had to wait until they were fired upon.

Seeing their missiles destroyed by the alien craft behind them didn't sit well with the American pilots. The weapons officer aboard the fighter chose to fire a missile backward at the craft. With an instinctual move of self-defense, Susan placed her hand on the weapons-control stone and attempted to dispatch the oncoming missile. What she didn't realize was that the pulse might continue forward and strike the aircraft. The tail section of the F-16 was vaporized shortly after the missile had been fired at the alien craft. The fighter was going down quickly, and the pilots shed their canopy and activated their ejection seats.

The parachutes deployed successfully; however, The Guardians didn't like the prospect of the Iraqi army descending on the pilots when they hit the ground. They envisioned their arrest and subsequent torture at the hands of the cruel Iraqi interrogators. They had to act fast. Kevin brought the craft directly underneath the falling parachutes and caught them one by one and gently lifted them higher in the air. He wasn't sure they had oxygen capabilities, so he kept his altitude under ten thousand feet and flew the pilots safely out of the no-fly zone back to their airbase in Saudi Arabia. They arrived with a slight case of windburn from the rough ride home, but for the most part returned unscathed. Their aircraft was in danger of crashing in a populated area, so Susan quickly dispatched it before it could hit the ground.

That night Iraqi television claimed that they shot down an American warplane and were confident that it was only the first of many more to come. The Guardians got a kick out of the claim. They imagined they could pay the Iraqis back by locating and dispatching their Al Samoud 2 missiles. According to the terms of the original United Nations resolution calling for Iraq to disarm all weapons of mass destruction, the Al Samoud 2 missile program was in direct violation. The U.N. resolution prohibited missiles that have a capability to travel in excess of one-hundred-fifty kilometers. The Al Samoud 2 missiles have the capacity to reach well over two hundred twenty kilometers; however, the Iraqis claim they plan to add a secondary guidance system, which would increase the weight, and therefore, decrease the effective striking range.

The Guardians thought this argument was full of holes and therefore, invalid. That was all it took. Less than three days later, all the Al Samoud 2 missiles were reduced to powder. The Iraqis claimed they had destroyed the missiles themselves and welcomed Franz Grover and his team of inspectors to substantiate their claim. In Washington, President Powell was livid. He was once again on the telephone to General Hightower at Patrick Air Force Base in Satellite Beach, Florida.

"Why won't the damned thing just let us have our war and get it over with," said Powell.

"I wish it was that easy, Mr. President. The Al Samoud 2 was our ticket to Baghdad. Now that they have been destroyed, we haven't a leg to stand on. There went our smoking gun."

"That's a fine song and dance, Steven," said the President. "But it still doesn't solve our problem. We have to remove Saddam, and if we do it alone, we stand to be responsible for bringing them back to the twenty-first century when we both know they were never there in the first place. We just don't have the resources. The attack on the World Trade Center and The Pentagon nearly collapsed us. The bastards still don't know how close they came. This country can't afford another 9-11."

"I know that Mr. President," said General Hightower.

"What else do you know? Tell me that, Steven. Tell me how we can get the U.N. to head into this action with us and not against us. What the hell's the matter with the French, can you tell me that? Jesus H. Christ, they sell a nuclear facility to Iraq just so the Israelis can blow it the hell up, then they offer to do it again. They'll sleep with anyone for money, those people. What are they standing to gain by opposing us, Steven? Why is Russia so supportive of France's unconscionable greed? So far our intelligence is anything but intelligent. The CIA is brain-dead, and the FBI is counting the days until they can start collecting their pensions. We've tied their hands too tightly, Steven. Now they're ineffective. What we need is a good old-fashioned assassination. Are we on the same page here, General?"

"I'm not sure we have a positive avenue for deployment," Mr. President."

"Speak English, Steven. This is an ultra-secure line."

"If you can find the bastard, I'll kill him for you," said the general. "Is that plain enough for you, Mr. President."

"That'll do, General. Oh, and just one more thing. The next time you want to print lies about Libya make sure that it accomplishes something. You failed to flush out your supposedly human space-pilots and succeeded in lighting a fire under one of the most dangerous son-of-a-bitches we've ever had to deal with. If Libya sponsors any more terrorist actions against Americans as a result of your slanderous brainstorming, it'll be your ass, General. Do we understand each other?"

"I read you loud and clear, Mr. President. Just trying to do my job," said the general.

"Well, try to do a *better* job, would you?"

"Yes, Mr. President." Hightower hung up the phone and said to Colonel Byrd, "I hate that guy."

"If it makes you feel any better, I didn't vote for him either, Steven."

Chapter Twenty-eight
July 30, 2005
9:00 A.M.
Melbourne Beach, Florida

The Guardians were enjoying a hearty breakfast after a hard night's work. They had just removed a major portion of the Egyptian Archeological Society's National Treasures Museum. They were running out of space at the house in Florida, so they took the artifacts to the moon. They placed them on a smooth crater floor in The Sea Of Tranquility where they could be identified by the Hubbell telescope. A quick telephone call to NASA headquarters using the computer voice would tell them where to look. Who knows, maybe it would entice Egypt to become a partner in the International Space Station. It could be a stepping stone for recovering a large part of their heritage. Susan had been in a dark mood for the past two days. She pressed Kevin for an answer he was unable to give, "What have we accomplished so far? The stock market is down thirty percent, the world is no closer to peace, and we're holding the only valuable contribution by man to this miserable planet for ransom."

"Oh, come on, Susan. The picture isn't that black. We destabilized a volatile situation along the borders of North and South Korea. How many lives did that save?"

"How many did it cost, Kevin?"

"I don't know, and I don't care. You think you can make us out to be the bad guys just because some capitalists lost a third of their advantage over everyone else," he argued.

"Some older people on fixed incomes lost a third of their life's savings. Was that also your plan?"

"Okay, say you're right. We haven't accomplished a thing. What now? Do we cave in and just say, *'go ahead and kill each other?'* That doesn't work either. The way I look at it, we're half way home. Once we can get the wealth restructured to ensure the welfare of all the people we can leave capitalism to resume its ugly devices. It'll be insider trading and unfair advantages galore. Martha Stewart can hold her head high again."

"Will *we* be able to hold our heads high, Kevin?"

"*I* will. If you won't then I guess I was wrong about you. I'm sorry I got you involved in the first place."

"I used to be afraid of getting pregnant," she said with a laugh. "Hell, I could handle that, but when you get a girl in trouble, *YOU REALLY GET A GIRL IN TROUBLE!*"

"At least I'm good at something," he said.

"You're good at a lot of things, Kevin. And you have a good heart."

"Thank you, Sue. It means a lot to me that someone knows who I am. I mean, that's the reason for all of this. To be who we are. To believe in what we think is right. Sure people have the right to abuse each other, but that doesn't mean we have to like it. And if we have the power to do something about it, maybe we can push them in a good way. For the good of the many."

"I feel a phone call coming on," said Susan.

"I think it's about time," said Kevin.

"Can they trace a cell phone?" she asked.

"Not if it's taped to a pay phone."

"But when they get to the pay phone, then what?" she asked.

"It disappears."

"Very clever these aliens," she said.

"We aim to please."

~

July 30, 2005
10:15 A.M.
Enfield, North Carolina

The Guardians found an unoccupied rest area on I-95 near a small town in North Carolina. The call could have come from anywhere in the country because The Guardians weren't concerned with the long distance charges. Their roaming was of an entirely different nature than the charges on a cell phone bill. Since it wasn't their phone, they wouldn't be getting the bill anyway. They dialed the NASA switchboard at Kennedy Space Center from the pay phone at the rest stop. Taped to the handset was a cell phone, which they then called with Kevin's personal cell phone. When the connection was made, they got back in the ship and traveled straight up to about three thousand feet.

"Kennedy Space Center," said the switchboard operator.

Kevin typed his phrase on the computer keyboard and pressed enter, *"This is a message for Mr. Sean O'Neal from The Guardians of the Way. We are the ones responsible for the destruction of the U.S.S. Valiant and the removal of your art treasures. We wish to speak directly with Mr. O'Neal at this time,"* said the mechanical voice.

"You'll have to schedule an appointment with Mr. O'Neal. He cannot be reached at this time," said the operator.

"Instruct Mr. O'Neal that we will reduce the orbit of the International Space Station by twenty miles in the next thirty minutes. The next time we attempt to contact Mr. O'Neal he will be available. That is all."

The Guardians then retrieved the cell phone from the pay phone at the rest stop. They would be using it again since the call wasn't long enough to trace. They then proceeded to Space Station Alpha. The ceiling of the clouds was at fifteen thousand feet. They broke through in an instant to a brightly-lit morning sky. Behind them the Earth fell away at twenty thousand miles per hour. The ship was capable of speeds much greater than that; however, they were in no hurry. They were hoping that word would somehow get through to the astronauts on Alpha and that the sudden repositioning of the station wouldn't startle them. When they reached the space station, they gently nudged it into a lower orbit by twenty miles. When they were through, Alpha was orbiting at two hundred twenty two miles. The normal operating altitude of the space station ranges from a maximum of two hundred fifty miles to a minimum of two hundred twenty. The orbit naturally decays at the rate of two and one-half miles per month. In their present position, the station had less than one month before it fell below the minimum orbit altitude. This immediately got the attention of the Director of Operations at the Space Center. He gave instructions to the switchboard to put The Guardians through to his personal phone line no matter what the circumstances. The Guardians had top priority regarding communications with the Space Center. The next time Kevin and Susan attempted the call, the outcome was quite different.

"This is Director O'Neal. Am I speaking with the Guardians?" he asked.

Kevin typed the reply, *"Yes. We are the Guardians. We have moved your space station to just above its minimum orbit altitude. As you know, its orbit will decay to the critical point within twenty-five days. We have the ability to increase its orbit up to the maximum or two hundred fifty miles. We do not desire to harm any of your space personnel; however, the maneuver was necessary to get your attention."*

"Well you've certainly gotten our attention. What are your demands?"

"We wish for the nations of Earth to restructure their socioeconomic hierarchies so all the people have adequate health care, housing and nourishment. That is all. This position is our only demand, and it is non-negotiable. Once the task is completed, all of your art treasures that we have taken will be returned to their rightful owners. As always, we will be watching. That is all."

Chapter Twenty-nine
July 30, 2005
11:04 A.M.
Kennedy Space Center

Director O'Neal was on the phone to the President in the Oval Office.

"I'm sure they mean business, Mr. President. We stand to lose the space station if we don't comply."

"I know, I know. Steven Hightower said he almost lost the B-2 the other day."

"My God," said the director. "What is that, ten billion for a stealth bomber?"

"I think it's more like fifteen," said the president.

"That buys a lot of health care and housing, Mr. President."

"Oh, there's no question that we'll comply. I just hope they stay the hell out of our way in the war against terrorism."

"Why can't we let them fight it for us?"

"Because it's our job, that's why. We were elected or appointed to do our jobs, Sean. I'm not about to lose sight of that for anyone, are you?"

"No, Mr. President."

"I'm addressing the nation tomorrow night to introduce a comprehensive health and housing plan to cover all the people in America who have slipped through the cracks, so to speak. The health care will bring us a giant-step closer to socialism, but we have no choice. We'll have subsidized education for health care workers with the proviso that they work within the system for six years on a military captain's salary before going into private practice. The general public will still address their health issues with a business-as-usual approach. They can pay for superior care if they choose to, but we have only been directed to provide adequate care and that's what we plan to do."

"What about the other countries, Mr. President? Are they taking the demands of The Guardians seriously?" asked the director.

"Probably not. Look at Africa. There are a lot of countries in Africa that can't do the right thing. They're too far gone. They can't feed themselves, clothe themselves, or provide shelter and health care. It doesn't matter what threats The Guardians make. It's simply a logistical impossibility," said the president.

"Then I'm sure that The Guardians will charge the rest of the nations with the task. The strong will end up helping the weak until everyone is taken care of."

"Spoken like a true communist, Mr. Director."

"I'm sorry you feel that way, Mr. President, but I'll tell you one thing. I'll do whatever it takes to get that space station back up to two hundred fifty miles above the Earth."

~

July 30, 2005
3:15 PM
Basra, Iraq

The Guardians had destroyed all of Iraq's Al Samoud-2 missiles, but the Iraqi government had told the United Nations weapons inspectors that they had done it themselves. When they were asked to show the dismantled parts to the weapons inspectors, they directed them to a large pile of rubble largely consisting of dust. The inspectors accused the Iraqi people of orchestrating a deception intended to stall the progress of the inspections. Washington was quick with their response. Kevin and Susan were in Melbourne Beach perusing the article in the local paper. The headline read: **"U.S. Jets Strike Five Targets in Southern Iraq."**

Associated Press

WASHINGTON – "U.S. warplanes patrolling a 'no fly' zone over southern Iraq reported coming under anti-aircraft artillery fire and responded by attacking four military communications facilities and one air defense facility," officials said Monday.

Central Command said in a statement that the attacks happened Sunday. The official Iraqi News Agency quoted an unnamed military spokesman as saying that six people were killed and 15 wounded in an air strike in Basra province Sunday.

"Our courageous anti–aircraft units confronted the warplanes and forced them to leave our skies toward their bases in Kuwait," it quoted him as saying. It called the targets "civilian and service installations."

The communications facilities were located near the city of Al Kut, and the air defense facility was near Basra. Those areas and others in southern Iraq are frequently targeted by U.S. planes because they are important links in Iraq's air defense network. Central Command said Sunday's attacks were ordered after Iraqi forces fired anti-aircraft artillery at U.S. and British planes.

"Here we go again," said Kevin. "I guess the U.S. and British planes haven't learned enough of a lesson. Let's take the ship over and destroy a couple billion dollars worth of aircraft, Susan."

"Come on Kevin, they'll only build more. We have to be careful, or we'll bankrupt most of the world's economy."

"But we have to make a statement, Sue. Six people killed, and 15 wounded. Remember the last time? Those planes were never really fired upon. That was a preemptive strike on their radar and anti-aircraft facilities. It wasn't self-defense, and I think they're playing the same game all over again."

Chapter Thirty
July 31, 2005
2:04 P.M.
Southern Iraq
'No Fly Zone'

The Guardians were poised at seventy thousand feet over the Basra Province in southern Iraq. Having arrived there an hour and a half earlier, Susan had been dozing on and off in her chair waiting for the American warplanes. Kevin was reading a book about sea life on the Great Barrier Reef of Australia. He was anxious to conclude their business with the British and American planes, so he could take Susan there and experience the region first hand.

A squadron of fighter-bombers passed beneath them at sixty thousand feet. Apparently, neither the radar of the warplanes nor the ground forces had detected them. When the planes dropped the first bombs of their sortie, Susan was quick to dispatch them. The Americans were quick to discover that their attack was being interfered with and tried to fire air to air missiles at the hovering spaceship. Susan was able to destabilize most of the missiles; however, one exploded very near their ship. Although the ship itself wasn't damaged, the concussion forced their bodies to the side with such force that they nearly lost consciousness. That's when they began to get angry at the warplanes.

"I'm done playing around," said Susan. There was a small trickle of blood evident on one of her earlobes. Seeing her blood served to incite a fury toward the American and British warplanes in Kevin. Susan dismantled them one by one, first clipping the wings so the startled pilots could eject with their parachutes intact. After the pilots had ejected, she methodically destroyed the remainders of their planes. There would be no safe ride back to their Saudi air base this time. They left the American and British pilots to fend for themselves on the hostile ground of southern Iraq.

"It serves them right, Kevin. They nearly knocked us out of our seats. I'm not sure, but I think that would cause our canopy to open and spill us out into the atmosphere at twenty thousand feet."

"Not a very nice scenario, Babe. I don't blame you for downing the planes. Let's just hope they learn a lesson this time."

"You know they won't."

"Then next time it'll cost them a lot more than a few planes," said Kevin. Susan had no doubt but that he meant every word of it.

July 31, 2005
5:00 P.M.
Kennedy Space Center

The Guardians had once again contacted Director Sean O'Neal at the Kennedy Space Center by phone. They were put through immediately.

"We have a request to facilitate our communication efforts that we hope you will comply with. We will give you a cell phone number that you may call to communicate to us. The original owner of the phone is of no consequence to you. We acquired it at a vista-point of your Grand Canyon. Someone abandoned the phone for a reason unknown to us. We shall use it to maintain contact with your world leaders. We hope this arrangement will be satisfactory with you."

"I understand," said the director. "I'll pass the number along to The President of the United States, if that is your wish."

"It is. We also require that the number to be given to General Hightower at Patrick Air Force Base and Admiral Carl Bender's office in the Naval Command Center located in the building you call The Pentagon. We have a specific message for both of them."

"I'll be happy to comply with your wishes," said the director. "May I ask a question please?"

"Yes, you may," said the mechanical voice.

"Are you able to increase the orbit of the Space Station Alpha to two hundred fifty miles?"

"We are."

"Will you do so? For the good of humanity?" asked the director.

"We have yet to see a positive direction for the good of humanity among your nations. We ask that you lead the way. Then we will help you in ways beyond your imagination."

"I'll try to convey your message to the appropriate people. I ask only that you remember that the personnel on the station are not military. They pose a threat to no one. They are merely scientists trying to make this world a better place to live."

"It will become a better place to live, Mr. O'Neal. Whether you wish for the change or not."

Kevin and Susan returned to their house in Melbourne Beach with a sense of hope for the first time since their confrontation with the world leaders began. They were getting pretty good at pushing the military around. Their play of force was escalating as expected, and soon they would be able to demonstrate an event of such catastrophic proportions that there could be no recourse but to heed the warnings of future reprisals. They had nothing else to do but to order a pizza and wait for the phone calls to come rolling in.

Chapter Thirty-one
July 31, 2005
5:10 P.M.
Patrick Air Force Base

General Hightower had just received the telephone number from Director O'Neal that would allow him to contact the Guardians. He reached for the phone and said to Colonel Byrd, "This is it, Clifford. This is where it hits the fan."

Then Kevin heard the cell phone ring and said to Susan, "Just like clockwork. Which one do you think it is?"

"The phone has caller ID," she said. "Check the display." Kevin could tell by the area code that it was a local number.

"It's Hightower," he said.

"Tell him I said, 'Hi,'" said Susan.

"Right," said Kevin sarcastically. He booted up the laptop computer and chose to speak in the voice called Zarvox. It was the same voice used by the famous Physicist Stephen W. Hawking to help him speak - a detail that was instrumental in making the choice.

He handed the phone to Susan, and she plugged a speakerphone cord into the microphone jack. That way they could listen to the speakerphone and then mute the cell phone while they discussed their answer. Susan would type the reply on the keypad and then activate the voice by choosing *'speak the selection.'*

"This is General Hightower at Patrick Air Force Base. Am I speaking to The Guardians?" he asked.

"Yes," was their reply.

"Are you responsible for destroying an entire squadron of U.S. and British aircraft earlier today over Iraq?"

"Certainly."

"Why?" asked the general.

"Their assault was pre-emptive, not self defense."

"We are preparing to go to war. We needed to knock out their communication centers to protect our armed forces," said the general.

Kevin and Susan left the phone muted while they discussed their next move. Kevin said, "You were right, Sue. They still don't get it. They think they're going to have a war. The great United States is going to smash a third world country to bits over oil and call it anti-terrorism."

"What do you think we should break next?" she asked Kevin. "How about the B-2 Stealth Bomber?"

"Sounds good to me. But make him sweat about it for a while. Tell him we're gonna' do it tomorrow."

"You got it," she said. Susan typed and sent the reply,

"There will be no war, General. We are surprised that you would even consider such an action in light of the demonstrations that we have provided you. Your species is caught in a deeply rooted predilection for violent behavior. We shall help you overcome it. Some time tomorrow your B-2 Stealth Bomber shall be destroyed. We are sure that will help you overcome your temptation to use it. Be assured that the next pre-emptive hostile move by your branch of the armed services shall result in the destruction of your entire inventory of Stealth Bombers. Next will be your Stealth Fighters, and then finally the F-22's. We will make sure that if you are determined to go to war, you will have to use your bare hands instead of weapons. That is all."

"Very nice, Sue," said Kevin after hanging up the phone. The next call was from the admiral in the Naval Command Center.

"This is Admiral Carl Bender at The Pentagon in Washington D. C. I was told to call this number to receive a message from The Guardians," said the admiral.

Susan typed and sent the reply, *"Please wait."* She and Kevin discussed their response to the Navy and decided on taking out a nuclear air craft carrier.

"What do you think," she asked. "Should we take out the Kennedy or the Roosevelt?"

"I liked Roosevelt better," said Kevin.

"You got it," she said.

Susan typed and sent the message: *"Admiral Bender. Your air craft carrier U.S.S. John F. Kennedy is currently deployed in The Gulf Of Oman. You will order all of your aircraft to launch from the carrier and instruct them to land at the air base in Al-Wakrah Kuwait."*

"Why would I do a damned fool thing like that?" asked the admiral.

"By five o'clock tomorrow afternoon there will be no U.S.S. John F. Kennedy. Be assured that any hostile pre-emptive attack by your branch of the armed services shall result in the destruction of your entire Sixth Fleet. That is all."

"Nicely done, Sue," said Kevin.

When the president called them, Kevin and Susan decided to make one last ploy in the hope that the world was not totally beyond redemption. The only thing larger than an air craft carrier that they could think of was an asteroid. They told the U.S. president that Earth's destruction was imminent due to its position in the path of an asteroid more than twenty-two miles wide. They said that by the time Earth's astronomers discover the asteroid, there will not be sufficient time to divert it. The point was further driven home by the fact that Earth didn't have the appropriate technology to move so great an object. The Guardians said that they had no hand in the event, which is destined to unfold. It is a natural occurrence for every celestial body over the course of time.

They also said that although they were not the cause of the asteroid's path, they did have the power to alter it. They could easily divert the asteroid into a harmless orbit around the sun. They said that the events they had witnessed during the last month had made them disinclined to interfere.

They suggested that perhaps the Creator of their world was having second thoughts. Fate alone had given the people of the Earth a rare second chance to survive a cataclysmic catastrophe. It was in their power to choose their own destiny. Only time would tell if they could learn from their mistakes. And, as always, they would be watching from the dark side of the moon.

Chapter Thirty-two
August 1, 2005
9:00 A.M.
Melbourne Beach, Florida

Following the destruction of the B-2 Stealth Bomber, the Air Force was standing down all pending missions over Iraq. They were in limbo and awaiting further instructions from the joint chiefs and the president. The Navy had launched all the planes from the carrier Kennedy. A skeleton crew was all that was left, and they also would be disembarking shortly. Kevin Murphy and Susan Lang were having breakfast and laughing about the look on General Hightower's face when the Stealth Bomber turned to dust. They felt that Admiral Bender's face would look very similar just after five o'clock this afternoon. Kevin took a news article out of his shirt pocket and handed it to Susan. He said to her, "Read this, Sue. I think it's one you missed."

Associated Press - Kenya The International Association of Geologists has reported that the Kumbala Diamond Mine, which was abandoned during the 1970s, is once again one of the country's major producers of gem quality diamonds. Abandoned for safety reasons due to a number of deadly cave-ins, the Kumbala Mine recently underwent a major geological transformation in the form of a series of oval tunnels traversing Mt. Kumbala overnight. Geologists are uncertain as to the cause of the transformation but are leaning toward the theory of a multiple sinkhole phenomenon. The Kenyan government has never sold the mineral rights to Mt. Kumbala so the hugely prolific mining operation stands to be a major source of revenue for the North African country.

Kevin reached into the pocket of his jeans and poured a handful of stones on the table in front of Susan.

"Are those what I think they are?" she asked.

"You bet. I've got about five pounds of them."

"Five pounds of diamonds?"

"Uncut diamonds. They're only worth about fifty mil."

"Fifty million dollars?"

"Give or take. You want me to give them back?"

"What are you nuts? Of course, not."

"I thought you'd say that. Finish your breakfast, Sue. It's almost five o'clock in The Gulf Of Oman. We've got a date with a big boat."

"Oh, that's right," she said whimsically. "A Guardian's work is never done!"

"Do you want to trash the Kennedy," asked Kevin.

"No thanks," said Susan. "I did the Valiant. It's your turn, Babe."

"You're so good to me. What did I do to deserve you?"

"You brought about the end of the world."

"I wouldn't say that," said Kevin.

"I would. The world we knew is gone. The world we knew had death and destruction for hire. Natural resources determined whether a people should live or die. That world is gone. Death for profit is a concept of the past. It's ancient history. Face it Kevin. You brought about the end of the world as we knew it."

"I promise, I'll never do it again."

"You know, I think you're making a lot of progress with your trust issues. We may soon be seeing the light at the end of the tunnel."

"Okay, then lets get married, dammit!"

"Oh, Kevin Darling. That's sooo romantic. I may just get a case of the vapors!"

"No, I mean it. I want to get married . . .I mean . . .will you marry me, Susan?"

"I thought you'd never ask."

Chapter Thirty-three
August 2, 2005
6:54 A.M.
Melbourne Beach, Florida

A black van drove slowly down the dirt road two miles west of I-95 in West Melbourne. The huge web of red lines that Susan Lang feared they were drawing finally led a highly trained black ops task force to the unattended ship. Although the men couldn't actually see the ship, they knew from the last heat vector where she lay, just under the surface of a small lake. Two of the men lifted small scuba tanks over their heads and adjusted their masks and snorkels. Seven minutes after they descended beneath the sleepy little lake, one of them surfaced and signaled to the other men with a thumbs up gesture. The search was over. The ship had been located and the control stone had been left in the port side cradle. All appeared to be lost for Kevin Murphy and Susan Lang.

Chapter Thirty-four
August 3, 2005
8:15 P.M.
Washington D C

"Yes, General. He's been expecting your call. I'll put you through, hold please."

"Hello, Steven," said the president. "Tell me some good news."

"We got it. At o-seven hundred this morning we located the craft in a lake by a pasture in West Melbourne, Florida. Thirteen hours later we had her bed down at Patrick. No incidence. Zero civilian observation as near as we can tell. The damn thing makes a vertical decent from ten thousand in about a minute."

"Outstanding," said the president. "Was it your men, Steven?"

"It was the Scorpions, Sir. They're still on site inspecting the now dry lakebed for artifacts."

"Which branch is that?" asked President Powell.

"None, Sir, they're civilian contractors."

"Mercenaries? Are you telling me that the United States armed forces uses mercenaries, General?"

"Actually, they don't exist, Sir."

"Who doesn't exist, Steven?"

"No one, Sir. The point is, we've got the ship."

"Don't shut me up, Hightower, I asked you a direct question. Who the hell doesn't exist?"

"Actually, the Scorpions are classified, Sir. We are their only contract. Outside of the work they do for us, they are compelled to stand down," said the general.

"We have a secret fifth branch of the armed services?"

"As I said, Sir, it's classifi. . ."

"Horseshit, Steven. I'm your commander and chief. Nothing is classified where I'm concerned. Do you read me, General?"

"You are the sitting President, Sir."

General Hightower's remark was clearly meant to drive home the point that there was little chance that the president would be re-elected in sixteen months because his handling of the conflict in Iraq was subject to a fair amount of criticism.

"I'll tell you where you can sit, Stevie boy." began the president, "Why don't you sit down nice and hard on your purple heart."

"Whatever you say, Sir."

"You bet your ass, whatever I say. And another thing; I'm gonna get a ride in that thing."

"But, Sir. . ."

"No buts, Hightower. Marine One's gonna put me at your doorstep first thing tomorrow. Look for the flight plan and arrange security, or your next tour of duty will be at a military academy. Do I make myself clear?"

"Clear as glass, Mr. President," said the general. Rather than hang up the handset, Hightower placed it gently on the table before him and silently left the room. As he reached the door, he could hear a faint voice coming from the desk, "Steven. . .Steven . . . ARE YOU THERE?"

Chapter Thirty-five
August 6, 2005
7:55 A.M.
Patrick Air Force Base

General Hightower's most gifted pilots worked for twelve straight hours being *tutored* by the machine's life-form interface properties. By 6:00 A.M. Lieutenant Andy Krausman was as certified as any pilot would become with respect to the strange ship from the cosmos. He rightly felt that, if needed, he could fly it through the eye of a needle. The only thing the young lieutenant couldn't do was remove the port side stone from its cradle. They had drained the lake and could open the ship, but they had no way to protect their precious treasure by hiding it with the control stone. The ship *told him* that there was another *pilot* who alone had the specific DNA required to remove the port-side stone. When he reached out with his mind, the ship was quick to *tell him* of the tragic events in the life of Coal-Eyed Joe and The Massacre at Indian Key; however, when he tried to learn the current pilot's identity, he came up empty. The security surrounding the small, insignificant dry lakebed in Florida was beginning to rival that of Area 51, the Roswell New Mexico crash site.

Andy Krausman, the craft's new pilot was instantly aware of the limitless capabilities of the alien craft. He was a quick study and was seriously considering resigning his commission. He was aware that along with his new found knowledge came an attitude change as well. He wasn't quite sure that it was for the better. He felt that, if nothing else, he needed to be extremely careful with respect to what he *asked* the ship to do. What the young lieutenant didn't account for was the foolhardy passenger that he was required to take along for the ride. President Powell arrived as promised to be one of the first to experience the extraordinary characteristics of the alien craft. When the president asked Lieutenant Krausman to fly six inches off the Indian Ocean at four times the speed of sound, he didn't realize that the ensuing tsunami would ravage the people of Sri Lanka, Indonesia, and India resulting in the death of over 230,000 people.

A shift in the Earth's mantle was said to be the cause, but Kevin Murphy and Susan Lang knew the truth. Their heart of hearts held them to blame for their carelessness. They had allowed the ship to get out of their hands and now the rest will be history. Their legacy was to become one of infamy, born of irresponsibility. So dark was their mood that it was a struggle to even rise from the bed in the morning.

"We've got to make it right, Kevin," said Susan.

"There's no way," said Kevin.

"There's always a way. We can't give up hope."

Just then Kevin heard a familiar scratching sound on the back yard sliders. It used to annoy him to no end, similar to fingernails being raked across a blackboard back in school. Somehow the sound was immensely appealing this time. He instantly knew what it meant. It was Misty. She'd come home again after her travels over the past two weeks.

They both rushed over to the door. Misty wagged her tail to tell Kevin how glad she was to be back home again. She would have also barked with delight, but for the fact that her mouth was presently full at the moment. It held a blue stone. It was the starboard side stone that Coal-Eyed Joe tried to scuttle along with the port side stone nearly a hundred and eighty years before. It was his belief that a mile out to sea was plenty of distance to assure that his fellow man could not gain control of the terrible force from the stars. He was wise enough to know that some powers are too perfect and can too easily bring out the evil side of man. Mankind would have to learn the hard way that a mile was not enough.

"That dog just saved the planet, Kevin."

"She helped, but now it's up to us. We have one more chance, actually it's more than we really deserve."

"We really screwed up, didn't we?"

"You think?" said Kevin sarcastically. "A quarter of a million souls are going to make my dreams a little crowded."

"Kevin, don't."

"What would you have me do, Sue, forget about it?"

"Don't let it ruin you, that's all."

"I'm already ruined. Both of us are. Listen to yourself, Sue. You don't want to take any responsibility."

"We can't bring them back, Kevin. I have to live with that, too. My life will never be the same. I'll never take a breath without feeling the pain that we have caused all because of that damned ship."

"Because of me, Sue."

"Oh, stop beating yourself up. Start thinking about making it right."

Kevin grabbed the stone off the coffee table and said, "You coming?"

"Lead the way."

Chapter Thirty-six
August 6, 2005
8:15 A.M.
Patrick Air Force Base

"A what?" screamed General Hightower. "A tsunami, sir. A large wave traveling at over two hundred miles per . . ."

"I know what a tsunami is, Lieutenant," said the general grabbing the young Lieutenant by the lapels. "I had your assurance that you had the damned thing under control."

"Yes, sir. I mean, no, sir. I did, sir, but the President, sir, he requested me to . . ."

"Kill thousands of people? Well, you did a very good job of it, didn't you?" he screamed. "I've got to get a handle on the damage control. If it ever gets out that we caused a . . ."

"A tsunami, sir," said Krausman sheepishly.

"A catastrophic weather phenomenon," he growled, "we'll give new meaning to the term The Great Satan, won't we?"

"Yes, sir," said the lieutenant.

The telephone on the desk began to ring. General Hightower just glared at it for a full thirty seconds before answering it, "Hightower," he said gruffly into the phone.

The President was intoxicated with his newfound power. He was beside himself with his excitement, "Steven! We just won the war, and we never even had to fire a shot."

"How many dead, Mr. President?" asked Hightower.

"Oh, who cares about the damned Indonesians? Don't you realize what this means, Steven? We can create weather as a weapon and not even be responsible. We're invincible and it happened on my watch!"

"I'll tell you what happened, Mr. President. On your watch we just made Hitler look like Mother Theresa. *If,* and I do mean *if* we can cover up this whole affair, we have to make sure that the United States is never connected with that evil contraption ever again."

"I'll expect your resignation on my desk within the next twenty-four hours, General," said the President.

"I don't think so, Powell. As far as I'm concerned, you can go piss up a rope," said the general.

"You're gambling with your pension, Steven. Are you sure you know what you're doing?" asked the President.

"Did you know that all phone calls to this facility are recorded? It's just like calling 911. Here let me play this back to you . . ." The general pressed a button on his telephone console and the President's voice could be heard loud and clearly over the line, "Oh, who cares about the damned Indonesians? Don't you realize what this means, Steven? We can create weather as a weapon and not even be responsible."

"Sound familiar, Powell?" asked the general.

"Have you ever heard of the term suicide by Secret Service?"

"I don't think so," said the general. "The tape is still rolling. I don't think you want another death on your hands."

"I'm thinking that the Air Force may not be the correct branch of our armed forces to dispatch our latest weapon," said the President.

"I'd send it to the moon if I could," said Hightower.

"You'd be tried for treason, Steven. I'd make sure of it," said the President.

Sergeant Ed Blue suddenly burst into the room, "General Hightower! The craft is moving!" he said as he ran over to the window and gestured with his outstretched hand.

"Who's in the cockpit, Sergeant?" asked the general.

"That's the point! The craft is empty, but it's moving away!" said Sergeant Blue.

"Well, I'll be damned," said the general with a chuckle in his voice. He returned his attention to the man on the other end of the phone line, "I don't think we have to worry about which branch of the services gets the craft Mr. President. I think the issue is being decided for us as we speak."

"What are you talking about, Steven?" asked the President.

"Our deliverance," said the general. "Deliverance."

August 7, 2010
9:37 P.M.
Melbourne Beach, Florida

It had taken The Guardians twenty-four hours to retrieve all the paintings, statues and jewels that they had stored on Earth's moon. Since the ship remained invisible, the artwork appeared to just materialize out of thin air in front of museum entrances and in the case of the *Crown Jewels of England,* the narrow stairway leading up to the Tower of London. In the dead of night, the burial mask of King Tut appeared on the desk of Zaphi Hannas, who was the chairman of the Supreme Council of Antiquities in Egypt. The Guardians no longer had the stomach to continue their fruitless efforts to control the will of mankind. They realized that even with their lofty values, they were no better than those they condemned. Evil is evil, no matter what face it wears. In the hands of its alien creators, the ship was a benign tool for influencing procreation. In the hands of man, it became only a method of destruction. No good would ever come of it. The technology would never match the level of maturity.

Chapter Thirty-seven
August 9, 2010
8:15 P.M.
Above The Mariana Trench
(Approximate depth seven miles)

T he Guardians had just finished their evening meal aboard the cruise ship *Coral Wonders*. After they returned all of the art treasures back to their rightful owners, they decided to scuttle the ship in the deepest section of the Earth's oceans. They sent it to the bottom of the Mariana Trench. There was no getting around the fact that no human should have control of the alien craft. The best intentions just weren't good enough. What was created to spread love and bring about proliferation of life turned to hate in the hands of man. The Guardians' final responsibility was to make sure that the craft would remain inaccessible to humans. It only took the U.S. military one day to inadvertently kill a quarter of a million people. But they weren't really to blame. They didn't know the awful truth behind the limitless capabilities of the alien craft. The Guardians knew and would forever pay the price of their carelessness. And they would forever bare the responsibility. After they tossed the control stone seven miles beneath the sea, there would be no possible way for it to be retrieved should anyone somehow learn where to look. They knew they couldn't trust themselves with the limitless power of the ship. Obviously, trusting anyone else was out of the question, also. The power-hungry human psyche was a recipe for disaster, there was just no getting around it.

They were alone on deck during a clear night in a calm sea. As they looked aft, they could see the slight luminescent quality of the water. It seemed to take on a lighted turquoise hue, which faded out a few hundred feet behind the ship. Susan took the control stone out of her purse and said, "This is it, Kevin, the moment of truth."

"Moment of sanity, at any rate," said Kevin.

"I love you, Kevin. Do you know that?"

"I know, Sue. I love you, too. I knew you'd talk me into this. I think that's why I chose to share it with you in the first place. You scared me for a moment when you said we had to keep the power accessible, but I knew you were too smart to take that chance."

"We were starting to lose ourselves, baby. Nothing's worth that."

"Not even the power of *The Guardians*?" he asked with a hint of shame in his tone.

"Having second thoughts?" she mused.

"No way."

"Let's go then." They looked around them to make sure they were alone, and then Susan said, "Someone's coming out the ballroom doors, here goes . . ."

Kevin saw a flash of blue from her outstretched hand as their terrible temptation sailed down into the sea. There were no regrets from either of them. There never would be. Kevin instantly felt a great weight lifted off of his shoulders. Their exhausted embrace melded into a final, triumphant sigh. *It was finally over! They were free!*

Chapter Thirty-eight

August 14, 2005

9:15 P.M.

Melbourne Beach, Florida

Kevin and Susan were sharing a fairly old bottle of Louis Martini Cabernet Sauvignon and eating warm Brie cheese with slithered almonds on wheat crackers. They both looked up, seemingly as one, to the spot where the fabulous painting had hung just a few days before.

"I can't believe we actually had it for a while. Was that cool or what?" asked Susan.

"Cool as a moose, honey," said Kevin. "I miss the Monet, too."

"Well, they're back where they belong. Maybe we can go visit them sometime," said Susan.

"Good idea."

Epilogue

Seven Months Later
March 10, 2006
8:15 A.M.
Melbourne Beach, Florida

Susan Lang has it all. She has a good and trusting man in Kevin Murphy, a good friend in Misty, and a good position at the Satellite Beach Center For Mental Wellness. She also has a new life growing inside of her. *What a fantastic adventure to live in these times.* She was bursting with anticipation over how her child would grow and change the world. He will have the power. It will be presented to him on his twenty-first birthday. A simple, little blue stone that looks surprisingly similar to the cell phone that she threw from a cruise ship the year before.

The End